To Dorothy & Ethel   6 June 2008
So delightful to meet another
    Birman family.
        With love from Susie x

OF CATS AND ANGELS

by
MR D'ARCY
a very special Birman Cat

with assistance from
SUSIE JACKSON BATTY

AuthorHouse™
1663 Liberty Drive, Suite 200
Bloomington, IN 47403
www.authorhouse.com
Phone: 1-800-839-8640

First published by AuthorHouse 2/27/2008

ISBN: 978-1-4343-5681-9 (sc)

Printed in the United States of America
Bloomington, Indiana

This book is printed on acid-free paper.

Also by **Susie Jackson Batty**

The Diary of the Lady from Devizes

authorHOUSE®

For 'Aunt' Doris

and all the friends who loved and looked after Mr d'Arcy and his sisters, Portia and Pandora, over the years. This book is a big thank you to all of you. It is also a love story.

Sometimes someone comes into one's life, who is so special that one's whole being is filled with love. I am so lucky because it has happened to me twice – the first time with Andrew, my darling husband of thirty-six years – the second time with my adorable Mr d'Arcy.

Producing this book for Mr d'Arcy has been an extraordinary, loving and spiritual experience. His words simply flowed and all I had to do was write them for him.

Susie Jackson Batty

The Legend of the Sacred Cats of Burma

Centuries ago in Burma the Temple of Lao-Tsun housed a golden goddess called Tsun-Kyan-Kse. She was very beautiful with sapphire blue eyes and she watched over the transmutation of souls. One of the priests at the Temple was Mun-Ha, who often knelt in meditation before the goddess with his cat, who was called Sinh, always at his side. The temple housed 100 white cats.

One night as the moon rose and Mun-Ha was kneeling before the sacred goddess, raiders attacked the temple and Mun-Ha was killed. At the moment of Mun-Ha's death, Sinh placed his feet upon his fallen master and faced the goddess. Immediately the white hairs of his body were as golden as the light radiating from the beautiful golden goddess, her blue eyes became his very own, and his four white legs shaded downwards to a velvety brown, but where his feet rested gently on his dead master, the whiteness remained white, thus donating their purity.

The next morning the temple radiated with the transformation of the 100 white cats which, like Sinh, reflected the golden hue of sunset. Seven days after his master's death Sinh also died, carrying with him into paradise the soul of Mun-Ha his beloved master.

☆   ☆   ☆

The Sacred Cats of Burma appeared in France at the beginning of the twentieth century, and the breed was recognized in France in 1925. British breeders started to raise Birmans in the 1960s and the breed was recognized there in 1966. These cats have a wonderful temperament. They are sweet, gentle and very loving. They are very beautiful and walk with a tiger-like gait.

Table of Contents

Portia

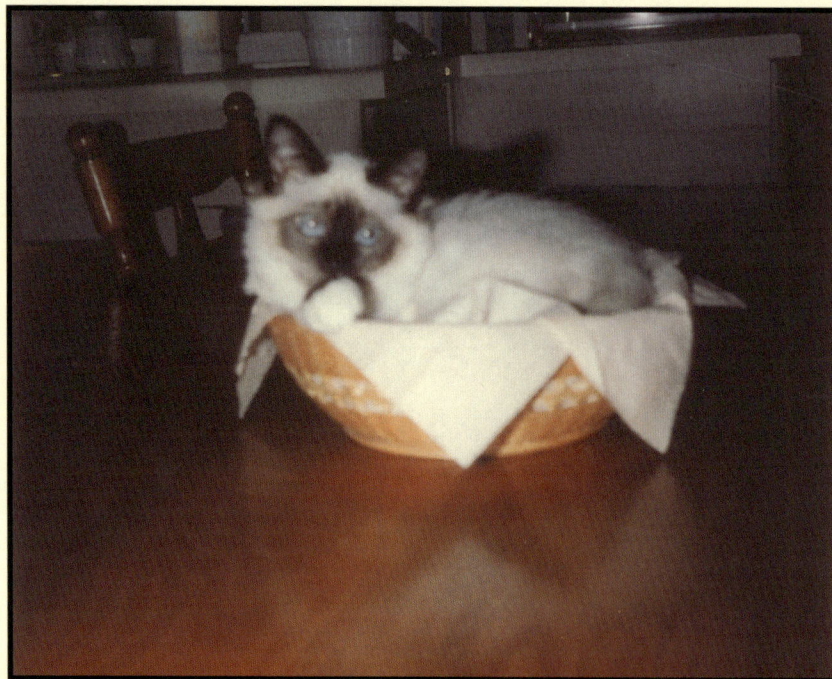

Pandora

Chapter One
Living at The Dolls' House

I love Susie. I have always loved Susie. I love Andrew too, and my sisters, Portia and Pandora, but I simply adore Susie. Ever since I came into her life seventeen years ago I have wanted to be with her every waking moment when she is at home. If she sits down I climb on to her lap. I love to climb up her chest and nuzzle her face. I love her so much I just want to eat her. In fact I get told off for doing 'lick, lick, bite' which is my favourite trick – two licks and then a little lovebite.

I was born on 2 April 1987 in Hitchin, Hertfordshire, England and my pedigree name is Vanbelma Storm Chaser. I am a very handsome Seal Point Birman with blue eyes and white paws. My parents, Champion Vanbelma Valaricki and Vanbelma Persephoni, lived with a Birman breeder in a big family of pedigree cats. We can trace our ancestors right back to the first Birmans in England and I have lots of champions on my pedigree. Pandora is also a Seal Point Birman and she came from the same family as me. Her pedigree name is Vanbelma Kevino Lily. Portia is a Blue Point Birman and she came from another family who lived nearby, and her pedigree name is Nefertari Gypsy's Pride. We all had the same father but different mothers.

I was a year older than Portia and Pandora, who were adopted by Susie and Andrew when they were tiny kittens. Birman kittens are born with completely cream

Andrew and the Kittens

A Kiss on the Nose

coloured fur and the colour pointing appears gradually as we grow. By the time Portia and Pandora went to live with Susie and Andrew they had some colouring appearing – in Pandora's case it was brown and in Portia's case it was blue. As Birmans grow to adulthood our full beauty appears.

I was first adopted by a young couple who adored me and called me Pixie. I had a happy life with them for the first year until a baby arrived in the family. I so wanted to be with the lady and the baby, but the couple were worried that I was too affectionate and they shut me outside in the garden. There were two mean-spirited Siamese cats living next door and they teased and taunted me, and I became very disorientated and I started spraying in the house – not a pleasant habit.

The couple had to return me to the breeder. I was glad to be back there with my family and I stopped spraying. At that time Susie and Andrew had just lost their Birman boy, who was called Oscar. They were very miserable and telephoned the breeder who told them about me. It was agreed that I would go to live with them for a week to see if I behaved myself and fitted in with their two Birman girls, who were of course my half-sisters.

Susie and Andrew came to meet me. They thought I was very beautiful with my blue eyes, cream coat, my very dark face, legs and tail, and white feet. They drove me to their house, which was about an hour away in Beaconsfield in Buckinghamshire. I was carried into the kitchen in the travelling box and they opened the door and let me out. Portia and Pandora greeted me and I explored my new home with them watching me.

Susie went out in the evening for a couple of hours and when she came home I was tucked up on the sofa next to Andrew and the two girls were on his lap. Susie was so thrilled to see that I was happy, and I felt very content immediately in this new home. Susie decided that Pixie was not a suitable name for a very handsome and sophisticated pedigree cat and she chose the name Mr d'Arcy for me. Many years ago she had fallen in love with Laurence Olivier when he played the part of Mr d'Arcy in Jane Austen's Pride and Prejudice. Amazingly many years later, Susie's cousin's son married the grand-daughter of Sir Laurence Olivier. So I became Mr d'Arcy and I certainly grew into this wonderful name.

Devoted Sisters

I join the family

The house where we lived was called The Dolls' House because that is what it looked like, with the front door in the middle and windows on each side. There was a small hall with a door on each side. The door on the left opened into the diningroom and on into the kitchen, and the door on the right opened into the sittingroom and also on into the kitchen, so when the doors were all open one could go round in a complete circle. The stairs to the upper floor were straight ahead of the front door. Susie and Andrew used to keep the doors to the hall closed so that if anyone came to the front door there was no danger of any of we three cats leaving the house by mistake.

At night Pandora, Portia and I were put to bed in the kitchen. Susie and Andrew knew that if we were allowed to be upstairs that they would have no peace all night as we would want to be snuggled in with them, giving them licks and lovebites too. Every morning we were so excited to hear movement and would wait for the doors to be opened and then we would dash upstairs and explore everywhere all over again, and then chase each other down the stairs ready to be brushed before breakfast. We all adored being brushed. The girls were always first and I would sit gazing adoringly at Susie waiting for my turn as she talked to us telling us how beautiful we were. My favourite part was having my tummy brushed when I would lie down on my back with my legs in the air.

There was a catflap in the kitchen door, which was locked at night. It took me a while to get used to using it, but after watching Portia and Panda pushing the flap up with their noses and climbing out, I soon managed to do it. Susie and Andrew had made a wonderful safe 'safari park' for us to play in, with a big tree in the middle for us to climb. There was high fencing all around with a gate at the far end to the rest of the big garden. We even had our own special house, which was a wooden cabin and was called 'Birman Hall'. This had a downstairs for the litterbox and a ramp up to the cabin, which had a very big comfortable bed and we three spent lots of time relaxing there. It was especially useful to keep us safe if there were any workmen at the house who might leave the back gate open by mistake, so sometimes we were locked safely inside Birman Hall.

Birman Hall

The Aerobic Centre

I was only unhappy when Susie and Andrew were working on the big vegetable garden and fruit bushes, which were right at the bottom of their big L-shaped garden. If I was awake and could not get to Susie or see her I was very upset and walked up and down the fence calling out as loudly as I could. She usually relented and came back to pacify me.

Portia, Pandora and I had another favourite place to sleep and that was up on the shelf at the back of the long garage in the apple boxes. We had to jump on to the bonnet of Susie's car and then we could jump directly on to the shelf and climb into the boxes.

Susie and I had a very special relationship and she didn't realise quite why for some time, but the reason is that Susie's father always said that he wanted to come back as a cat. Susie's father died in 1980 – seven years before I was born. One day I was sitting up in one of the apple boxes when Susie came to look for me. It was a beautiful day and the sun was shining brightly in through the garage door. Susie stood and looked up at me and gasped "Mr d'Arcy, you have the same china blue eyes that Daddy had." I looked at her and **said** "Haven't you realised who I am yet……?"

☆   ☆   ☆

We had such a lovely life living with Susie and Andrew. We were thoroughly spoiled and greatly admired by all the visitors to The Dolls' House. We three were good company for each other. We all had different characters. Pandora was the boss, and Portia and I usually let her have her way. We had a wonderful three-storey stand in the kitchen, known as the aerobic centre. It had large square shelves on three levels and a tube supported by strong legs wrapped in thick string for sharpening our claws. It was a great game to see who could stay on the top shelf before being pushed off by the other two. We also had wonderful chasing games round the garden, in through the catflap making Susie jump, and round the diningroom or sittingroom. We were told off if we jumped all over the furniture and we were not allowed up on the kitchen surfaces – except in the night when there was no-one to tell us off and we could sit looking out of the window.

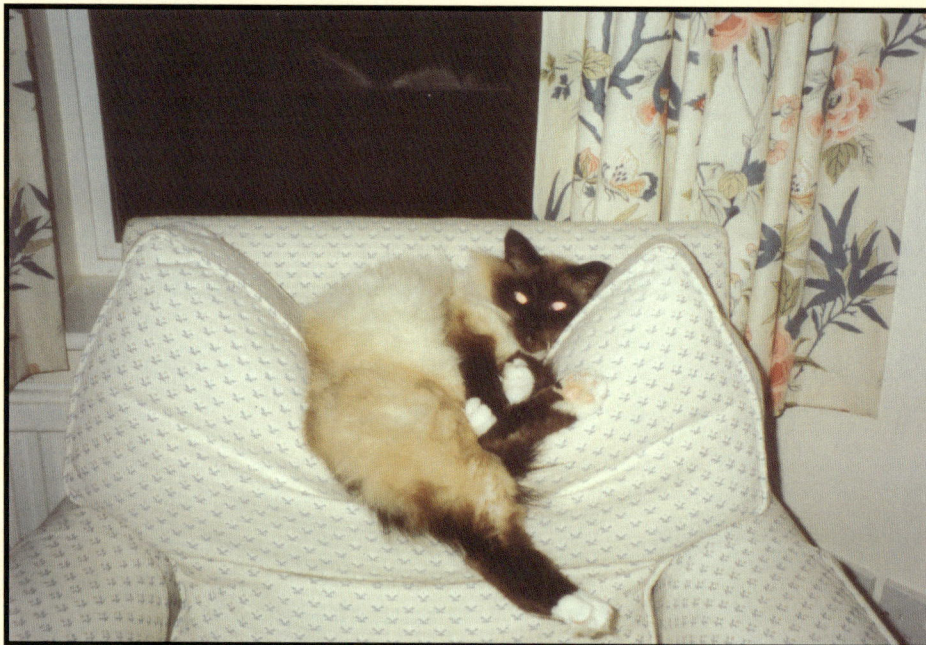

I Can Sleep Anywhere !

Each morning Andrew used to leave quite early and was gone all day, except for Saturdays and Sundays. We knew that he had a big job in the city called London, and he had a long journey to get there. He used to leave the house on foot by himself in the mornings walking down the drive, unless it was raining and then Susie used to drive him in the car for the first part of his journey. He used to catch a train from Beaconsfield into London. Susie would rush back into the house and hurry to get herself ready to go to her own job, returning each morning around lunchtime. In the evenings Susie always went to meet Andrew and bring him home. Sometimes the train would be late and they would both arrive home cold, tired and hungry.

We often heard Susie telling her friends about her job. She was private secretary to a wonderful gentleman called Lord Burnham and each morning she went to his beautiful enormous home, which was close by, and helped him with his work. One day Lord and Lady Burnham came to tea at The Dolls' House. Susie introduced us to them, and Lord Burnham asked her if she had decorated the house to match the cats or had got the cats to match the décor, which was very amusing. I suppose we did blend in with the cream carpet and the dark wood furniture. Lady Burnham said 'Oh Susie, this is such a sweet little house. Would you like to swop with me and live in my huge home? I could be so happy living here in The Dolls' House.' I pricked up my ears at this, and was relieved when Susie said laughingly 'No, I don't think so.' We enjoyed hearing Susie telling Andrew about her mornings with Lord Burnham over dinner each evening.

The catflap was locked when Susie was out, so Portia, Panda and I used to settle down in our beds in the kitchen until Susie returned. Then it was time to venture out to stretch our legs and explore our territory to make sure that everything was still where it was supposed to be. Susie often disappeared during the afternoon returning with lots of bags of shopping. When it was all put away she would join us in the garden and I always came running to the bench where she sat. She always talked to me, telling me all about her thoughts and worries, and what was happening in our lives.

My favourite time of day was the evening. After we had our tea and a stroll in the garden, Susie and Andrew would have dinner and then afterwards we would all move into the sittingroom to watch the magic box called a television. Now I am quite a bright fellow but I had no idea how the box worked, but it was entertaining to watch it sometimes, although we three usually fell asleep quite soon. The other mysterious object in the house was called a telephone. It made a loud ringing noise and then Susie or Andrew would speak into it. They would have a strange one-way conversation and then turn it off again.

When we were all ready to settle down for the evening on the sofa, Susie and Andrew would have to remember to have near to hand the telephone, the small box with the buttons to turn the television on and off and their evening coffee. As soon as they sat on the sofa we three would climb on too. Portia liked to sit on Susie's lap, Pandora liked to sit on Andrew's lap and I liked to climb up Susie's chest and give her a lick before she gently pushed me down on to her left hip and I sat half on the sofa and half on her hip, and she held my front paws in her hand.

Whenever Susie and Andrew were at home for the evening that was our routine. Of course they often went out to see friends, or their friends came to The Dolls' House to see them. Panda loved all the visitors. She loved everyone and wanted to be picked up and snuggled as much as possible. Portia was a little more reserved and didn't mind being stroked. I didn't mind either, as long as Susie was with me to reassure me.

One day during our first summer together, Susie and Andrew took us in our baskets in the car on a short drive to a place called Willow Cattery. We were greeted by the owners - a mother and daughter called Rita and Nicky. We were installed into a cabin, which was just like Birman Hall. Susie and Andrew stroked us and told us to be good. They said that they would be back in two weeks, and then they said goodbye and left us there. Apparently they were going somewhere which was a very long way away from The Dolls' House. We were looked after very well at our 'hotel'. It was made up of a long row of Birman Halls in a building near a house, and although we would have preferred to stay at The Dolls' House, it was not too bad. We were altogether in one large cabin. The only problem was that Pandora was horrified to see other cats and she screamed at the one in the next cabin. Now Birmans can really scream very very loudly, and she upset all the other cats in the cabins at first and had to be pacified by the owners.

That first time we had to stay at Willow Cattery I worried all the time that Susie would not come back for me, but the owners kept reassuring us that we were just on our holidays and we would be going home soon. I tried to settle down and in fact found it quite interesting to see the other cats, and also the other creatures which appeared at night, including hedgehogs, rabbits, mice, and even badgers, foxes and deer. My favourite was an old badger who came snuffling along most evenings.

It was the most wonderful moment after what seemed like a very long time when I heard Susie's voice again. She had come back for me! I was so excited. Portia and Pandora were put into their carrying basket and I was put into mine and Andrew drove us all home to The Dolls' House. We all talked all the way home telling them about our holiday, and they said how much they had missed us. They carried us into the kitchen and let us out of our baskets. Naturally we had to be a bit aloof at first and we walked around the room with our tails in the air. Then the back door was opened and we forgot to be aloof and chased each other out into the garden. We explored everywhere checking that everything was as it should be, and then we rushed back into the house. Susie picked me up and I put my paws round her neck and licked her face and my heart was full. I had missed her so much.

☆   ☆   ☆

There were always plenty of visitors to The Dolls' House. Susie and Andrew had so many friends, and sometimes family members came to stay. Susie's mother came to stay quite often. She was rather a strange lady and we thought that she didn't have much of a sense of humour. She enjoyed something called knitting and she kept pulling a long piece of wool out of a bag and clicking two needles. We thought this was a wonderful game just to amuse us and we would leap on the wool. She didn't think it was at all funny and eventually she gave up her knitting when we were awake.

Of course Pandora wanted to sit on her lap, but she just waved her arm about saying 'I don't want you, I don't want you'. Well, that didn't work with Panda, who jumped on to the sofa and when the right moment came just climbed on to her lap and gazed at her purring loudly. Even Susie's mother could not resist this clever treatment and gave in. Susie did try to tell Pandora that not everyone wished to have a cat on her lap, but Panda simply did not believe her.

On a couple of occasions during our early years at The Dolls' House, Andrew's very nice aunt and uncle came to stay. Auntie Barbara and Uncle Gordon lived a long way away and they came to look after us whilst Susie and Andrew went away on holiday. Although of course I was unhappy without Susie, we liked Auntie Barbara and Uncle Gordon very much because they were such kind and gentle people, who made such a fuss of us. They really enjoyed staying at The Dolls' House and strolling around Beaconsfield.

Eventually they were too old to travel from their home and we did not see them again. In fact Susie and Andrew were very sad one evening several years later to take a telephone call from Andrew's sister Jill, who told them that Uncle Gordon had just died. Then a very strange thing happened in the middle of that night. We were all in our beds in the kitchen and suddenly the room was filled with light and we all woke up to see the figure of Uncle Gordon gliding through the closed door from the kitchen to the diningroom. Now Birmans, being very spiritual cats, are familiar with these strange happenings, but Susie wasn't. I heard her on the telephone the next day trying to explain to Jill that she had woken up suddenly in the night and had looked towards the bedroom door and there was a beautiful glowing light about six feet high full of sparkling mosaic colours. Uncle Gordon's voice came from the middle of the light saying 'I have come to say goodbye – you were very kind to me'.......and then the light faded away.

Chapter Two
Susie and Portia are ill

We were very happy at The Dolls' House and we loved being out in our big garden, especially when Susie was out there too working hard weeding or trimming the shrubs. In the spring she had a big job to do planting all the tubs and hanging baskets. The garden looked wonderful with so much colour all through the summer. Each evening during hot weather she had to water everything, which took a long time but she was very conscientious and the plants flourished. Andrew's job was to mow the grass and trim the edges which he did most weekends.

The spring and summer weather was very changeable. Sometimes it rained for days on end, and other times it was very warm – there seemed to be no pattern to it at all. Occasionally Susie and Andrew invited friends to The Dolls' House for what they called a barbeque, which meant that Andrew was going to cook the food outside on a big grill. So often by the evening of that day the weather had deteriorated into grey drizzle and sometimes Andrew stoically cooked outside under a large umbrella. On those occasions the plans for eating outside had to be changed and the party had to be moved into the big kitchen instead. Susie used to get so disappointed when this happened and would groan about the dreary English climate.

Pandora Sunbathing.

This is Fun!

Susie liked to keep fit and one day she came home with a large box. She unpacked it with us watching. It contained a step with three levels. The empty box was very interesting and we all tried to climb inside it. Then she took the step into the sittingroom and put it in front of the television. She went upstairs, so we all went upstairs too of course, and she changed her clothes. Then we all came downstairs again, and she put on some special music and started stepping up and down in time to the music. This was very exciting to watch and I was enjoying it except that I desperately wanted Susie to pick me up, and I started protesting in a loud voice. She gave in and picked me up and we both bounced up and down to the music, until Susie gasped 'Dear Mr d'Arcy, this is far too much for me.   You are too heavy and you'll have to go down until I have finished my exercise.' She put me down on the floor and continued, but I jumped on to the step and got under her feet, so I was banished to the kitchen, which was such a shame because I was so enjoying it.

Susie liked to do her exercise to the music a few times a week and she always started off when we were asleep in our beds in the kitchen. She would quietly shut the door and play the music softly, but I always woke up and made such a fuss on the other side of the door that she relented a few times and held me while she jumped up and down. I really enjoyed her step routine.

We lived at The Dolls' House very happily for a lot of years and then some things happened to change our lives. The first worrying thing that happened was that Susie had a health problem and had to have some surgery. She had to go into hospital. We knew what that was like because each year we had to go to the animal hospital to have our routine injections to keep us healthy. Also sometimes one of us had an eye or mouth infection and we had to see the vet and have horrible medicine. However this was more serious as it was possible that Susie had something called breast cancer, which apparently could be a very big problem.

We listened to Susie and Andrew talking, and we knew that she was frightened. Andrew was very reassuring and strong and told her that she was in good hands. After a few days she had the surgery and was away overnight. Andrew had been to see her in the hospital and he told us that she was recovering well and would be home the next day. That evening we were all unsettled and kept getting under Andrew's feet in the kitchen while he prepared our tea and then his own meal. It was very strange without Susie and we were all rather subdued as we settled down for the evening.

Andrew brought Susie home the next day. I was overjoyed to see her. She rested on the sofa and we all wanted to comfort her, especially me of course. She had to put a pillow on her chest to protect herself from our efforts to sit on her and climb up to give her a kiss. She had to take it easy for a few days. We knew from what we heard that she was having to wait for a week for some results after the surgery. This was an anxious time for all of us, and we were so happy when she was told that everything was all right by her doctor. She was reassured that she would not have to have any more surgery, but she had to take a pill a day for the next five years. I thought that was very daunting, as none of us were any good at all at taking pills. Whenever Susie and Andrew attempted to give us a pill we would wriggle as much as possible, and if they managed to get it into our mouths we usually pretended to swallow it and then when they thought they had succeeded we would spit it out.

Susie had lots of visitors at this time, and the telephone didn't stop ringing. All her friends were concerned and glad for her that the news was good. Her sister, Kate, lived nearby with her Boxer dog called Nora. Whenever Kate and Nora Dog came to The Dolls' House we had to be in the house or in Birman Hall because Nora Dog loved to chase a tennis ball in the garden. Someone had to throw it first of all and then she would rush after it and carry it round in her mouth, or she would attempt to dig it into the grass with her sharp claws. Andrew was not keen on this activity, as patches would appear all over his lawn.

☆　　　☆　　　☆

One day when Susie and Andrew were out and we three were asleep in our beds in the kitchen, we heard a loud thud outside the kitchen door. Suddenly a strange man was looking in through the window at us. He had climbed over the high solid garden gate and jumped down just outside the kitchen door. We sat up immediately to see what was going on, and we were horrified to hear a window breaking at the back of the sittingroom. Then the door opened and the man came into the kitchen looking all around. We knew that something was very wrong.

The man ignored us and went back into the sittingroom. We heard him moving around and opening cupboard doors and removing things. Then we heard him open the door to the front hall and climb the stairs. He made a lot of noise in the big bedroom, opening drawers and throwing things out, and then he came back downstairs, and in through the diningroom where he opened cupboards and drawers again. He opened the door to the kitchen and came in carrying several bags. He looked at us again. We were scared but we tried to look unconcerned and we all started to wash, at the same time keeping an eye on the man. Cats always wash if something strange happens. Our parents always told us 'If in doubt wash'.

The man went back into the diningroom shutting the door behind him and he opened the front door and we heard his footsteps crunching on the gravel driveway. We stayed very still for a while, and then Portia decided to investigate the sittingroom as the man had left the door open. Panda and I followed.   The doors to all the cupboards were open and several things were lying on the floor and the sofas. We had a good look into everything and then we jumped out of the window into the garden and carefully looked around. We came back into the house and decided to go back to sleep. We had had enough excitement for one day.

Later on when Susie came home she tried to unlock the front door as usual, but it was already unlocked. This was a shock to her so she looked in through the front windows of the long sittingroom and she could see that Portia was in the sittingroom, where she was not supposed to be, but also that the window at the back of the room was hanging off its hinges. She knew immediately that there had been a burglary and she hurried into the house to see if we were safe. We all talked at once about the frightening man, and Susie looked all around the house to see the mess that he had left. She noticed immediately that several lovely things were missing, and then she telephoned Andrew to tell him that we had been burgled. She told him that we were all safe which was such a relief all round.

Susie started to make a list of all the items that were taken and she was so sad. When Andrew came home she told him that most of their Silver Wedding presents had gone, as well as several inherited treasures and items of jewellery, which were irreplaceable. They were very angry and upset. The next day a policeman came to the house and we were introduced to him as he admired us very much. Susie said again that she was so relieved that we were all safe. The policeman made notes but warned that it was doubtful that the burglar would be caught, or that any of the missing items would be found.

☆ ☆ ☆

The next upsetting thing to happen was that Portia started sneezing a lot, so after a couple of days Susie took her to the animal hospital. The vet said that she had a cold and gave her some pills. Susie groaned, as we are all so bad at taking pills. It became a real struggle to try to get the pills into Portia, and Susie and Andrew tried to find tempting food in which to conceal the medicine. Several days went by and Portia was no better. Susie took her back to the animal hospital and the vet gave her different pills to try. It was a worrying time, and then even more worrying for us was the fact that Susie's health problem returned. She had to see several doctors over a few days, and then we had the really bad news that she would have to have major surgery and would have to be in hospital for a week.

This was all so worrying because we heard friends say words like 'breast cancer is life-threatening' and 'this is very serious' when Susie wasn't in the room. I was sitting on her lap one afternoon and I was so worried because Susie started crying. She said 'Oh Mr D, I'm so frightened, but the doctor says that he can take out the bad things in my breast and put something good back in.' Then she smiled through her tears and said 'My breast will still be there - it will just have different stuffing.' Then she took a deep breath and said "Mr D, we just have to believe in our hearts that everything will be all right. I shall just have to put this into the box in my head and shut the lid until I have to deal with it again.'

That night I prayed to all the spirits of the Sacred Cats of Burma to give me strength to comfort Susie, and especially to the Goddess Tsun Kyan Tse. 'Oh dear Goddess, please don't let Susie die.' How would I live without my Susie. I must be strong like Andrew and fill her with confidence that everything will be all right.

☆   ☆   ☆

The following weekend we had some interesting visitors who had come from another country far away called America. We were introduced to them and they were called Gary, Butch, Glenn and Martha. They made a great fuss of us. Then Kate and Nora Dog arrived too, so we had to be put into Birman Hall so that silly Nora Dog could do her trick of chasing the tennis ball round the garden. The weather was glorious that weekend and they were able to have tea outside in the garden. Susie had prepared a traditional English tea for them and they were very enthusiastic about the cucumber sandwiches, scones with jam and cream and strawberries.

Susie and Andrew had decided not to tell these friends about her impending surgery. Glenn was in a wheelchair because he could not walk without aid, and after they had left Susie was holding me and she said 'You see d'Arcy darling, my health problem is nothing compared to Glenn's difficult life.'

After a few days Susie said goodbye to us and told us to be good, and that she would be home again in a few days. She gave Portia an extra cuddle because she was worried about her. Andrew took her to the hospital again and although he was very confident and strong in front of her we knew that he was very worried too. That evening we all curled up together on the sofa and Andrew tried to reassure us that everything would be okay and Susie would be home soon. During the next few days he had so much to do, because apart from looking after us and visiting Susie in the hospital, there were so many telephone calls from family and friends. They hadn't told many people because they wanted to keep it to themselves and the immediate family, but even so Andrew still had lots of calls from such kind people, including the Burnham family. Susie would not be able to go to her job for some time to come. It would depend on how soon she recovered from the surgery.

The days passed and Susie came home. Of course we were all overjoyed to see her, especially me. Andrew had bought a dozen red roses and they were in a vase on the table ready for her. She walked in with Andrew helping her and was delighted to see the roses. She was very weak and wobbly and Andrew helped her to sit on the sofa with her feet on the stool. We all talked to her and jumped on to the sofa and she had to have a pillow in front of her again. I just had to climb on to the back of the sofa so that I could reach down and give her a lick, and she cried and said how she had missed us all so much.

That night we all went to bed feeling happier that Susie was home, and then in the early morning hours another very strange thing happened. The kitchen was suddenly filled with a wonderful glowing light and we all jumped and sat up in our beds. It was an angel – a lovely man who told us that he was Raphael, Susie's Guardian Angel. He was beautiful and very tall with shoulder length hair and big white wings. He wore a long robe in a most wonderful glowing blue colour. He told us not to be frightened, and we weren't at all – in fact we felt such a wonderful comforting feeling. He said that he had come to give Susie some strength and confidence, and we were so glad. He passed through the door and we didn't see him again that night.

The next morning Susie was different. It was difficult to explain, but she was much calmer. I heard her on the telephone talking to Kate telling her that she had been woken in the early hours by three cool breaths on her cheek which made her feel so peaceful, and that she had found a small white feather on her nightstand. She said with a smile that it must have been her Guardian Angel, because it was not Andrew as he was in a different bedroom, and the cats were downstairs. I knew from this that she could not actually see Raphael, but I was so very glad that he had been to comfort her.

Andrew stayed at home for the next few days, taking care of Susie and of us. Kate came too and helped with meals and ironing. The surgery had taken a lot out of Susie and she had no appetite and she had lost some weight. She was also very bruised and we were so shocked when we saw her without her clothes. The bruising was all over her top half and she had white bandages all over one side of her chest. She had to go back to see the doctor several times and then a nurse starting coming to the house every day to change the dressings on Susie's breast. She continued to lose weight and we were all worried, but she said that she was pleased as she had always wanted to be a bit slimmer.

During this time Portia was still very unwell and Andrew had to take her back to see the vet several times. The problem in her nose had become worse and her breathing was very noisy. She became quite distressed at times and could not get comfortable to sleep. I heard Andrew tell Susie that the vet had suggested possible surgery and treatment for Portia, but that the vet was not very hopeful of a successful outcome and that it was probably not right to put her through it. This was very shocking for me and I didn't tell Pandora or of course Portia.

Susie and Andrew were desolate about Portia. This stressful time was not helping with Susie's recovery and she was still very weak. Kind friends came to help with shopping and other things during the daytime when Andrew was not at home. Someone came every day, and sometimes several friends and Kate came all at the same time. The days passed with lots of appointments with doctors for Susie. One day she came home with Andrew and she was very emotional, but this time the tears were of happiness because she had been told that she would not have to have some awful treatment, which she had been dreading. Apparently she had good results after the big surgery and this treatment was not necessary. We were all cheered by this – some good news at last.

☆   ☆   ☆

As the weeks went on Susie gained her strength and recovered quite well, but very sadly our darling Portia became worse, and Susie and Andrew had to make a very hard decision. They took her to the animal hospital and the Vet gave her something to make her sleep forever. Susie and Andrew had cried all the way home and they brought Portia into the kitchen to show Panda and me. She was curled up on a towel and Panda walked round her and then I gave her a kiss. Susie and Andrew took her to the bottom of the garden and had a little ceremony. It was such a sad time and we were all so miserable about losing Portia.

Soon after that we went to stay at Willow Cattery again. It was strange not having Portia with us, and Rita and Nicky were sad for us. We had heard Susie and Andrew telling their friends about another home that they had somewhere far away in the sunshine. This was where they went when they left us at the Cattery each time. When they returned this time they were very excited to see us again, and they told us that sometime in the future we might all go together to this other home, which was in a place called Florida. We didn't really understand at the time, but we heard them telling their friends that they were seriously thinking of making long-term plans to move to another country. This all sounded very scary to Pandora and me and we didn't want to think about it. It had been so upsetting to lose Portia and we just wanted to settle down again back home at The Dolls' House.

It wasn't long before Susie had to go back into hospital for some more surgery. She told us that it wasn't so serious this time and we were not to worry about her. She was away for three nights and then Andrew brought her home again. It was very worrying to see her because she was exhausted and she had lost more weight. The bruising was all over her top half again. Apparently she was bleeding internally again just like the last time, and this time she had a long tube coming out of the side of her breast with a large bottle attached to it to drain the bleeding. I heard her telling Kate that her doctor was mystified by her excessive bleeding, and that he had told her that he had never had a patient like her before in all his years of being a surgeon.

She had to see the doctor every day in the hope that the drain could be removed, but each time she came home with the horrible drain still in place. It was a miserable time for her but she tried to carry on as normal. She would dress and push the long tube down into her jeans and then put the large bottle into a carrier bag and attach it to her belt. She had to rest for several days and when she gained some strength back she would go out shopping with her attachment concealed under her clothes. She needed lots of love and licks, and we were not allowed to climb up her chest. Panda sat on her lap and I sat as close as possible to her and rested my paws against her thigh which was very comforting for both of us.

One night after a particularly trying day for Susie, when she was very fed up with the drain problem, Raphael made us all jump by suddenly appearing again in the kitchen. We were so glad to see that wonderful being, and the next day Susie was much calmer again. I heard her telling Kate that she had felt the three cool breaths on her cheek again in the night, and that she had found another feather. She said "I know it was my Guardian Angel. I don't know how I know, but I know that his name is Raphael." We were so thrilled to hear her say that, and I gave Panda a knowing look.

It had been a very trying time for Susie and finally after about three weeks she came home rejoicing because the drain had actually been removed. She gave us both a big hug and said that she felt wonderful. She would now be able to wear her clothes tucked in at the waist and life would be much easier again. Unfortunately all the internal bleeding had apparently caused a lot more problems so Susie knew that she would have to have even more surgery in the future to put the problems right.

For this reason she had decided that she would not be able to return to her job. She was very sad about it because she had been with the Burnham family for sixteen years, but it was the right decision as someone else had been helping the family while she was recovering, and that person was available to stay on in her job. Susie went to see the family to say goodbye and she was very delighted to be given a beautiful gold bracelet with elephants round it as her retirement present. She was told that she could of course still visit the family and enjoy walking in the vast grounds of the big house in the future. Susie and Kate and Nora Dog had often taken walks there over the years.

Snow!

Keeping warm

Chapter Three
Leaving The Dolls' House

The next time that we went to stay at Willow Cattery was in the middle of winter. The weather was very cold and Rita and Nicky said that they were very jealous of Susie and Andrew being able to fly away to the sunshine. Fortunately the cabins were heated and we had heated pads in our beds too so we were quite cosy. After we had been there for a couple of days it started to snow and we were fascinated by the falling snowflakes. After a while all the trees and flowerbeds were covered and everything looked so different. We didn't see many of the night creatures that time. Rita and Nicky worked as quickly as possible to clean the cabins and feed us all twice a day and brush our coats. Every cabin was full because this was a busy time. It was too cold for them to stay to play with us and we all slept as much as possible.

Susie and Andrew found it terribly cold when they came back from their holiday. They told Rita and Nicky that they had left bright sunshine and blue skies behind. Andrew had to drive very carefully on the way back to The Dolls' House because of the weather conditions. He said that he wished he was still in Florida in the sunshine, and Susie agreed. We were thrilled to be back home and when Susie opened the back door it was fascinating to see the garden completely covered in snow. Pandora gingerly stepped down on to the step with one paw but she quickly reversed. I tried it too but the snow was too deep. Fortunately it only lasted for a few more days and then we were able to go out for a walk in our garden, but it was too cold to spend any time in Birman Hall as it was unheated.

☆　　　☆　　　☆

That year we were glad when the spring arrived. It had been a very cold winter. Susie and Andrew told their friends that they had decided that life was too short to continue to endure the English climate when they had another home in the sunshine in Florida. They said that Susie's illness had been a life-changing experience for them and that Andrew had decided to give up his big job so that they could spend most of their time in Florida. They said that they had bought a florist shop to qualify for a visa so that they could live there year round. Pandora and I did not understand and were very worried by this news, and although Susie reassured us that everything was going to be wonderful, we were very unsettled.

We were very shocked when we heard them telling friends that if they were going to spend most of their time in Florida, they would have to sell The Dolls' House and just keep a smaller home in England without a big garden. Pandora and I were stunned - how could they think of selling our lovely Dolls' House and our garden with Birman Hall, and our big tree and all our secret places in the shrubs and everything? We didn't know what to think at this time, and then one day Susie came home and she was so excited. She told us that she had found a beautiful apartment on the River Thames and that we might be moving to live there.

When Andrew came home that evening she showed him a picture of this possible new home. She said that it used to be called Andrews Boatyard where boats were made, and it had been changed into a development of small apartments and was now called Andrews Reach. They laughed and said that it must be an omen to have that name. The next day they went to see it together and Andrew came home just as excited as Susie and they told us that they had bought this new home for all of us. Panda and I were shocked, but when I thought about it later, I said to myself that as long as I was with Susie wherever we lived   everything would be all right.

The next few months were so busy. Everything happened all at once. Susie had to have more surgery and she was in hospital for three days again. When she came home this time she wasn't so weak as the surgeon had given her some strong pills to prevent the bleeding. She was quite emotional though, which was worrying and when she was cuddling me the tears came. She said "Don't worry d'Arcy darling, it is just all the pills I have to take. I'll be fine soon."

She didn't have much time to recover because people kept coming to view The Dolls' House to see if they wanted to buy it. One couple were very taken with it and they decided to go ahead but they had to sell their own house first. Panda and I were very unhappy at this time, and it was a very stressful time all round because Susie and Andrew had to wait for this couple to sell before they could definitely agree to buy The Dolls' House. The other complication was that they were going away to Florida again and so wanted everything to be agreed before they went, but this was not to be.

We were taken to Willow Cattery again for another two-week stay, and when Susie and Andrew collected us at the end of that time they were still worried about everything because they were still waiting for the sale of The Dolls' House to go through. It had also been a very worrying time for them, as on the day that they had been due to travel on their big journey Susie had had a bleeding problem and had to have surgery instead of travelling that day. On our first day back at The Dolls House I was horrified when Susie told me that it had been touch and go as to whether they went away at all, because she had been in hospital for three days. Susie in hospital and I hadn't even known about it. When she told me this I cuddled even closer to her and she told me that finally her doctor had said that she would be okay to travel and they had eventually left. She said "D'you know Mr D, I had been so worried about everything, and then Raphael came to calm me down. I felt those three cool breaths on my cheek one night and then the next morning there was a small white feather on my nightstand. It was so wonderful – he was in Florida with me too.' I was so glad to hear her tell me that, and it was probably just as well that I hadn't known about her emergency.

☆   ☆   ☆

After a few more weeks of anxiety Susie and Andrew finally heard that everything had been agreed and they told us that we were definitely going to move to Andrews Reach. The moving date was fixed for two weeks' time and so the hard work of sorting out and packing up everything began. This was quite interesting for Panda and me because there were all sorts of boxes and bags to explore, and cupboard doors were left open and we went into everywhere and sometimes were shut in by mistake. It was exhausting for Susie and she had to take lots of rests, and of course we enjoyed resting with her. Andrew had to clear out the garage and he gave away most of his gardening tools. He said that it was going to be wonderful not having to mow the lawns any more.

He had to clear the loft out as well and he climbed up a ladder and disappeared. We were not allowed to climb the ladder and we were disappointed because the loft looked a very interesting place. Andrew passed things down to Susie and everything was so dusty. Susie opened a box and found her wedding dress from many years ago. She immediately tried it on, and found that it was too big for her.

As the days went on the house was full of boxes and bags ready for the move. The day before the move we were taken to Willow Cattery. Susie explained that we would be there for two days and then they would come for us and we would go to our new home. She assured us that we would find Andrews Reach very interesting, but Panda and I were very unhappy and unsettled not knowing what to expect.

The two days passed and Susie and Andrew collected us and drove us to Andrews Reach. The journey was twice as far as going home to The Dolls' House. Although we were apprehensive we were quite excited now to see this new home. Andrew drove through big gates and parked the car. They carried us in our baskets past some garages and down a path past some attractive buildings, then up four steps to two front doors. Susie opened the door on the right and we all went inside and down a narrow hallway past two bedrooms, through some glass doors and into a big room.

They carried us into a kitchen and Andrew shut the door. We were let out of our baskets and we immediately explored this long narrow room. Susie and Andrew were stroking us and reassuring us that all was well. Then the telephone rang and Andrew opened the door so we all went out into the big square room, which had a dining table and chairs and sofas. It was all the furniture from The Dolls' House and we jumped on to the familiar sofas and then down again to continue exploring our new home. There were glass doors and we could see through them to a balcony and beyond that to a lawn, which went right down to a wide stretch of water.

Susie showed us that our big bed and litter box and tray of food were all under the kitchen table. We both climbed into bed and started washing to calm ourselves and we were soon ready to start exploring again. There was a big pile of boxes on one side of the big room and Susie and Andrew were emptying them and trying to find places for everything. I decided that it was time for a nap and I fell asleep on the mat in front of the balcony doors with my legs in the air. The sun was streaming in through the doors and Susie decided to carry Panda and me into one of the bedrooms so that she could open the balcony doors.

Later at bedtime we were put into our big bed in the kitchen and the door was shut. The next day after breakfast Susie and Andrew decided to let us explore the balcony. We soon discovered that we could squeeze through the wooden struts and jump down on to the grass. Susie and Andrew followed us and they had two harnesses and leads for us to wear to keep us safe. Susie attempted to put one on Panda while Andrew held me, but Panda just rolled on her back and wriggled out of it. That wasn't going to work, so then Susie tried with a collar and lead. That was successful and so Andrew did the same with me. We all set off slowly across the grass towards the water. Panda and I were crouching and walking carefully and looking all around because this was all so new for us.

Andrews Reach from the other side of the River Thames

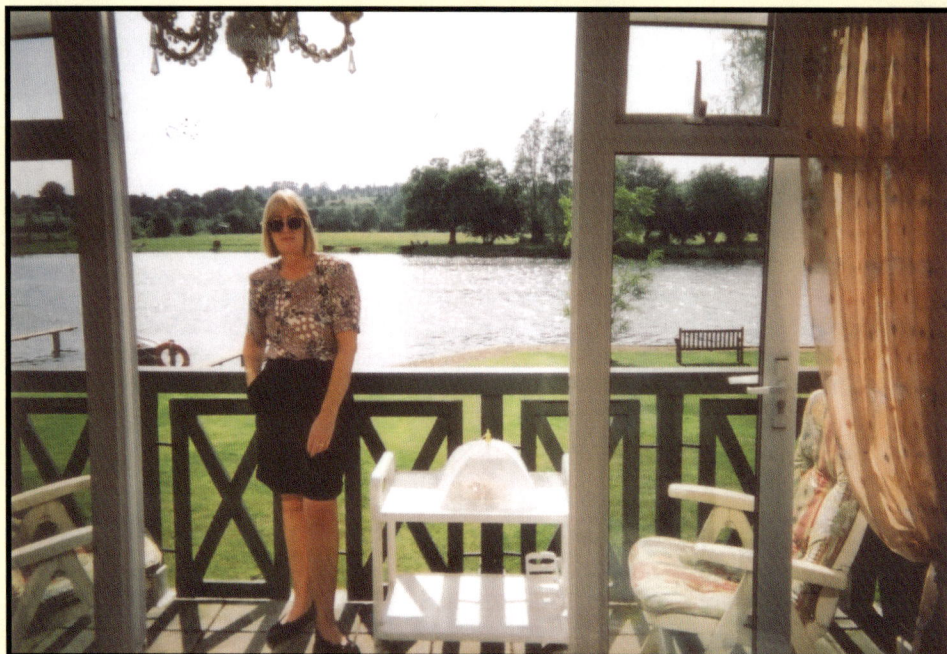

The Balcony and Our Bench

We arrived at the edge of the water and Susie told us that this was the River Thames. We were fascinated to see several boats going by slowly. On the opposite bank of the river there were people walking dogs, and in the distance we could see hills and trees. It was all very interesting and although it was very strange wearing a collar and lead we began to feel more confident. There was a wooden bench on the edge of the riverbank and Susie and Andrew sat down and lifted us on to their laps. To the left was a row of moorings with one boat tied there. A pair of coots was busy building a nest under one of the moorings and they were continuously bringing twigs in their beaks and dropping them into the nest. It looked like very hard work to me. A swan came swimming up which caused consternation and the coots shrieked at him.

A neighbour from one of the other apartments called Ann came to introduce herself, and then two other neighbours called Christine and Nick came down to the water's edge pulling a small boat on a trailer. They pushed the boat into the water and left the trailer on the grass. They waved to us and moved off along the river. It was really interesting watching all of this going on, but then it was time for us to return to the apartment so that Susie and Andrew could get on with the unpacking.

When we were put to bed in the kitchen that evening Panda and I decided that perhaps it was going to be all right living at Andrews Reach, although we were very sad about leaving The Dolls' House.

Chapter Four
Living at Andrews Reach

As the weeks passed by we became used to our new routine. Andrew still left each morning and returned in the evening. Susie did different things each day and she had lots of girlfriends who visited. They all loved coming to Andrews Reach and we enjoyed being admired and stroked. We grew to love our walks in the gardens. When Susie was on her own she could only take one of us out at a time because we always wanted to go in different directions, and we wouldn't walk together on our leads. One day Susie and I had been out for a walk and it started to rain, so we hurried back into the apartment just in time before the rain became torrential. Panda had woken up from her nap and decided that she wanted to go for a walk. She marched up to the front door. Susie opened the door to show her that it was pouring with rain, so she marched through the apartment to the balcony door and Susie had to open that one to show her that it was raining there too.

Every evening after Susie and Andrew had finished their dinner we would be waiting at the door to have our leads attached. Andrew would often take me because I always had to explore all the interesting shrubs by the big gates and Andrew had to go with me climbing over plants and round trees and touring the whole estate. He was so good about waiting patiently for me to move to the next interesting place, but he sometimes said 'Do come on Mr d'Arcy – let's go down to the river'. Susie took Panda because she only wanted to go straight down to the river, so Susie and Andrew would say goodbye to each other with a smile at the door, and we would all meet up again by the bench at the water's edge. We enjoyed sitting there watching the boats going by. People don't realise how their voices carry over water, and we often heard people saying 'Ooh, those cats are on leads!'

There were always lots of people walking dogs on the other side of the river on the towpath. Fortunately there was no path on our side of the river as our gardens went right down to the water, so we were not in danger of meeting any dogs, except Nora Dog when she came to visit with Kate. The weekends were especially busy with lots of boats on the river and walkers on the other side. Sometimes very big boats came by with lots of people partying on board, and we could hear loud music and everyone would wave to us.

The Sailing Boat

The Paddlesteamer

There was plenty of wild life to watch too. Lots of ducks visited often and there was a big flock of Egyptian geese, which someone said had escaped from a wildlife centre. Mr and Mrs Swan had a family of six cygnets and it was fascinating to see them grow up as the weeks went on. Susie and Andrew took bread with them each evening to feed all these visitors. They were careful to keep us back from the water's edge when the Swan family were visiting as the parents would hiss at us and we were a bit scared of them.

There was also a Great Crested Grebe, which was often swimming near the moorings. Susie said that she was sorry to see it on its own all the time. Then one day, joy of joys, the Great Crested Grebe had another Great Crested Grebe swimming with it, and they were bobbing and bowing to each other. From then on they were always together and were so entertaining to watch.

We became used to seeing several dogs, which were regularly walked on the opposite bank of the river. The water was shallow there and people would throw sticks and the dogs would leap into the water to retrieve them. It was fun to sit on the bench on our side of the river and watch all the excitement on the other bank. We also enjoyed seeing all the boats that came by, and we recognised lots of regular ones. There were some very large ones, which were sometimes crowded with people and at other times they had only a few people on board. There were lots of long narrow boats, some with clothes hanging from a washing line and lots of tubs of flowers. There was a beautiful sailing boat with a big cream sail that came by most weeks with a single lady skilfully guiding it back and forth across the river.

At the weekends the Sailing Club from Cookham, which was just round a bend in the river, sent their dinghies on races up the river and round a buoy, which was across from our balcony, and back again. It was fun to see these little boats with their pretty sails jostling for position. Sometimes one of them tipped over and the occupants had to scramble back on board after righting the boat.

☆　　☆　　☆

In the middle of that summer two of Susie and Andrew's friends came to visit. They had come all the way from Florida where Susie and Andrew had their other home. They were called Joan and Virginia and we were very excited to meet them. They thought that the apartment was 'cute and adorable'. When they were shown the River Thames, they said 'Call that a river !' They said that rivers in their country were huge.

Susie and Andrew told them that they were going to stay at The George Hotel in Old Beaconsfield, and that it was very very old, dating back to the fifteenth century. They gasped and Virginia said that they were thrilled because nothing in their country was very old, which seemed rather strange to me.

One day when Joan and Virginia were visiting with us at Andrews Reach, it was a very hot day and some people were swimming in the river from the other side. Joan and Virginia were horrified to see this and Joan said 'You British are desperate !'

That evening Virginia offered to take me for my walk whilst Susie took Panda, and Andrew and Joan watched from the balcony. They were so amused to see ME take Virginia for MY walk on my usual route through the shrubs and under the branches of the trees towards the big gates. Virginia called out to Susie who came hurrying with Pandora in her arms, and they swopped us over so that Virginia could just go down to the river with Panda. Susie and I went the long way round as usual and then we met up with the other two on the bench at the water's edge. Virginia was chuckling and said that cat-walking was a very interesting experience.

We saw them a few more times during the next two weeks, and then we were surprised when they said goodbye to us and that they would see us in Florida in two months. Panda and I were puzzled about this until Susie told us later that she was so excited because we were all going to have a very big adventure – we were going to fly to a new life in Florida. Well, of course, that sounded ridiculous to Panda and me – how could we possibly fly anywhere – only birds could fly, not cats and people !

We decided to ignore that news because we were quite happy with our new life at Andrews Reach in our nice home and enjoying our lovely walks. However Susie continued to talk about it with Kate, and her friends, and on the telephone with her mother.

The next week we were taken to the Animal Hospital. We waited until it was our turn and then the vet greeted us saying 'So you are all off on a big adventure to a new life – wish I was going with you.' He said he would check me over first and he stroked me and looked into my mouth and my eyes, ears, and everywhere. He said that I was a fine healthy boy and that the rabies injection should be no problem. Then he stuck something sharp in under my skin, which hurt and then it stung. It was horrid, and then he put something else into the back of my neck with a click, and he said 'There Mr d'Arcy, you are now micro-chipped .' I didn't know what that meant but I was very glad to be put back into my basket. Then it was Pandora's turn and she was most unhappy. The vet managed to examine her but she was very wriggly and he called for an assistant to hold her for the rest. Eventually we were ready to leave. The vet said that we should return in a month to see if the rabies injections had taken.

On the way home Susie said that she was sorry that we had to go through that horrid business, but it had to be done for our passports so that we could go on our big adventure. This was all sounding very worrying to Panda and me – we really did not know what to make of it, but Susie was very reassuring that everything would be all right.

The month passed quickly, and we were taken back to see the vet. It was a horrid experience because he shaved some of the fur from our legs and inserted a needle and drew some blood into a tube. He said that he hoped that all would be well and that he would telephone with the results in two days. We were very cross in the car on the way home to Andrews Reach and we both complained loudly. Susie said 'I know you didn't enjoy that experience, my poor darlings, but it had to be done.' We had extra treats and lots of cuddles that evening.

Two days later I heard Susie talking to the vet on the telephone, saying that she was so relieved that the results were good and the tests did not have to be repeated. When Andrew came home she told him what the vet had said and later when they were having their dinner they clinked their glasses of wine together and they laughed and said 'Here's to Florida'.

Chapter Five
The Big Adventure

The next few days were very busy. Suitcases appeared, and whenever they appeared it was always a worrying sign that life was going to change in some way. One evening when Susie and Andrew had taken us for our walks and we were sitting on the bench by the river, Susie said 'I am going to miss Andrews Reach so much.' Andrew replied that it wouldn't be forever and they would be back to stay here again. Susie said 'Yes, but Mr d'Arcy and Panda won't be coming back here again.' Panda looked at me and we were both shocked. Whatever was going to happen to us?

The very next day our lives certainly changed and the big adventure that Susie and Andrew had spoken about started. After breakfast we noticed that the suitcases were by the front door, and Andrew appeared from outside with two large carriers. He put Pandora into one, and me into the other one. There was a lot of room inside my carrier and one of my toys was in there too. Andrew carried the suitcases outside and then came back for us. Susie locked the front door, and we all went down the path to the car park. We were put into the back of a small red car. It wasn't Andrew's big Jaguar because apparently he had sold it the day before and rented this little car.

We set off and drove for a long time. Susie and Andrew talked to us during the journey and tried to reassure us that everything was all right, but I could tell from Susie's voice that she was anxious. After some time Andrew stopped the car and turned off the engine. They both got out of the car and Andrew lifted the suitcases out and then our carriers. Susie had wheeled a trolley to the car and everything was put on to it, including us in our carriers. Andrew hurriedly wheeled the trolley into a building and told Susie to wait there while he returned the rental car.

He rushed off and Susie knelt down and opened the door of my carrier and put a bowl of dry food into it and also a bowl of water. She did the same for Panda. She was talking to us all the time in a soothing voice, but I knew she was pretending to be calm. I looked out of the door of my carrier and saw that this was a very large busy place with lots of people walking in different directions. There was a lot of noise too and it was very worrying. Several people, mostly ladies, stopped to admire us and talk to us. Andrew came hurrying back and the trolley started to move again as he pushed it.

We arrived at a desk and a lady asked several questions. She told Andrew to push the trolley over to another row of desks and we waited for a while and then a man arrived to talk to Susie and Andrew. He said that he had come for the kitties. Susie said 'They will be all right, won't they?' He replied 'Don't you worry ma'am – I shall look after them.' Andrew said 'Bye bye Panda – be good – see you in Florida.' Then Susie said goodbye to me. She said 'Be a good boy Mr D, and everything will be fine.' I could tell that she was trying not to cry, which was very worrying. Andrew put his arm round her to comfort her.

The man wheeled us away on the trolley down some long corridors and into a large room. There were some other carriers in there but we couldn't see the occupants, although we could hear some strange noises. The man lifted our carriers on to a shelf and said 'Won't be long kitties.' Then he shouted to another man 'These cats are for the Delta flight to Atlanta.' The other man came over and said 'Okay mate.' We waited for a long time and nothing happened. Pandora called out to me and I answered her and tried to sound calm.

After ages and ages the second man lifted our carriers on to another trolley and wheeled us down more corridors and through a door to the outside. We could see an enormous shape ahead of us and it was making a very loud noise. The man lifted our carriers on to a moving platform and shouted to another man 'Here are the cats mate.' We went up a steep slope and I slipped down to the bottom of my carrier. I called out to Panda and she had too. The platform levelled off and my carrier was yanked to one side and then carried a few feet before being lifted up on to a shelf. A man tied straps round the carrier and secured it on both sides.

I could see Panda's carrier arriving next to mine. The man secured hers too and then he shouted that everything was on board and a big door was slammed shut. It was quite gloomy in this big room and difficult to see very much of anything. I was hungry and ate some of my food, and very thirsty and I had a big drink. I shouted to Panda to eat something and drink some water. She shouted back that she had lost her appetite but that she had had some water.

We sat there in the gloom for quite a while wondering about the strange loud noises, and I worried that I wouldn't see Susie ever again. Then we felt as if we were moving and we were. This big place was moving and then it stopped and after a moment it started moving in the opposite direction for quite a while. Then the noise increased and was terribly loud. It was very frightening and I crouched down as low as I could. Suddenly we started rushing along at such a speed and then our carriers were tilted and I slid sideways to the end of the carrier. I hit the side and stayed there stuck.

I was so frightened, my ears were popping and I could hear Panda calling to me. I was too terrified to speak and I wet my trousers. Then we seemed to level off and I was able to get my balance and move myself into the middle of the carrier again away from the wet part of the cushion. I stayed crouched for ages afraid to move, and then amazingly I fell asleep. I woke up after a while and the noise was still the same – just a loud drone. It went on for hours. I hoped that Panda was okay. I called out in a low voice but she didn't answer.

So it went on – sleeping and waking for hours. What was happening and where was Susie? After a very long time I heard the noise changing and I felt that I was being tilted again but in the opposite direction. After some time the noise increased to screaming pitch and suddenly we were being bumped and my head hit the top of the carrier. I felt dizzy and awful and thought I was going to be sick. My heart was racing and I was so frightened. I just lay there hoping it would be over soon and that Susie would rescue me.

Then the big room slowed right down and moved gently for quite a long time and it was quieter. After a while it felt as if we had stopped moving and suddenly the big door to the outside was opened and several men came inside.   I don't remember much more but Panda told me afterwards that we were moved from that big room down the moving platform and on to a trolley, which was wheeled into a big building. She said that we had to wait for ages and then Susie and Andrew came and found us. Susie was very upset to see me lying on my side and not moving. She opened the door of the carrier and stroked me trying to soothe me, but I just couldn't respond to her then. I felt so awful, and I smelt worse. Susie closed the door and kept talking to me while Andrew put our carriers on to another trolley and then we were wheeled through more corridors.

I started to feel a little better and thought that maybe I would live after all. I heard Andrew asking someone where he should put our carriers. A man said 'Just put them on the conveyor belt with the rest of the baggage.' Susie gasped and said 'Are you sure that there's someone to look after them through the flaps?' The man said there was. Susie said, in a tearful voice, "I can't do that' and Andrew said 'We have no choice. It will be all right, and we must hurry or we will miss the next flight.' So we were parted from Susie and Andrew again, and horror of horrors we were put on to another moving platform. I vaguely remember my carrier being pulled off the platform and carried into another big gloomy room, and then strapped on to another shelf with all the awful noise again. The whole terrifying experience was repeated and after a while we found we were rushing at high speed and being tilted until the room levelled off again. I could not believe that this was happening again and thought that Susie had abandoned me.

The noise became a drone and I called out to Panda. She answered in a very small voice. At least she had survived this far. I didn't know what to think and all I could do was to try to sleep. Then it didn't seem very long before the room started to make different noises again and I knew that it was tilting again.   I called out to Panda to hold on, and we both slid to the end of our carriers. Suddenly we were being bumped again but not so badly as the time before, and then the room made the loud screaming noise and then it was slowing down and moving along at a gentler pace until it finally came to a halt.

After a while the door to the outside was opened and we heard lots of strange noises and then two men came and unstrapped the carriers. The one who lifted my carrier down said 'Pooh, what a smelly kitty' and I felt so embarrassed. Again we were put on to a moving platform and then on to a trolley. I was wondering what would happen next and was feeling very anxious, when we were wheeled through a door into a very big room with lots of people milling about. I felt a little better and I was sitting up and looking out, and suddenly I saw Susie. She and Andrew came hurrying over to us and thanked the man who had delivered us to them.

Oh, such joy, to see Susie again. She opened the door and stroked me. She had tears in her eyes and she said 'Thank goodness, you are all right Mr D. We were so worried about you and there you are sitting up and that awful ordeal is over now.' Boy, was I glad to hear her say that and I licked her hand. Andrew said that he would get the luggage and Susie waited with us, and then we were wheeled through a door to the outside. There was a big white car waiting for us and we were loaded inside with Susie and Andrew sitting just in front of us. The driver was a lady and she asked where we were from. Andrew told her of our journey and Panda and I joined in telling them all about our ordeal. The lady laughed and said 'What wonderful talking cats.' Susie said 'I think they are saying that they don't want to do that again.' Too right !

Chapter Six
We are Floridians

It was only a short drive in the car and then we were being carried into a house. We were left in our carriers for a few minutes and then we were moved into a room. The door to the room was closed and Susie and Andrew opened the doors of our carriers and we came out slowly looking around us. Susie showed us our food and water containers and two nice beds and two litter boxes, one each. We both had a drink of water. Susie said 'This is your room now, and you won't be travelling anywhere else – you are Floridians now.' We didn't know what that meant, but we were just so glad to be with Susie and Andrew again. They opened the door to the room and we followed them out along a short passageway. Panda went straight on with Andrew, and I went into the next room, which was a bathroom. Susie said 'Now Mr D, let's clean you up' and she lifted me into the bath and ran the water and washed my fur. I didn't like that very much but I was glad to be smelling nicer again. Susie wrapped me in a big towel and held me very close. It was so wonderful to be in her arms again. She dried me and then let me walk out of the bathroom.

I came into a big room containing sofas and small tables, and in one area was a large table and chairs. Susie walked past me to some big glass sliding doors and said 'Come over here Mr D.' I could see Andrew and Panda outside by a big pool full of water.

I went out through the doors and walked slowly to the edge of the water and then I leant right over and had a drink of the water. Susie said 'Oh no, he's going to fall into the swimming pool', but I didn't. Then Panda and I explored all round the big pool. There was a walkway all round it and the whole area was covered with a big structure with see-through material, which wasn't glass because the air came through it. It was an outside room and there were long beds and a table and chairs. It was all jolly interesting.

It began to get dark and we were all very tired after such an exhausting day. Susie carried me and Andrew carried Panda back into our room and we both had some food and water and then we climbed into our new beds and settled down. Susie and Andrew stroked us and told us that everything was all right now and that we were all safe in our new home. They said goodnight to us and they closed the door. We both fell asleep immediately. I woke a few times in the night but I was able to go back to sleep because I felt safe in my new bed with Panda next to me in hers.

The next morning the door opened and Susie came into the room. We both climbed out of our beds immediately and walked out through the door. Susie lifted up our tray of food and followed us out. I went through the big room and out through the sliding doors to the pool. I leant over the edge and had a drink with Susie watching me closely. She said 'I wish you wouldn't do that d'Arcy darling – you are bound to fall into the water one day.' Andrew was busy freshening up the litter boxes and Susie put fresh food and water on the tray. Then it was time for us to be brushed. Susie knelt down on the carpet and Panda was first as usual, and I was waiting as close as possible and I rubbed my head against Susie's cheek while I waited, and she told us how beautiful we were and how wonderful we were, and we were so happy. We both adored being brushed, and I especially loved having my tummy brushed, and then being cuddled and kissed afterwards. It was just such a relief to be altogether again after the frightening experiences of yesterday. Susie said again that our travelling days were over and we were going to be so happy in this house in the sunshine.

Susie in the swimming pool

A Chap Needs a Nap

We were taken back to our room for our breakfast and Susie said 'See you later' and Andrew shut the door. We settled down for a nap and it didn't seem long before the door was opened again and Susie was there talking to us. We were ready for some more exploring and followed Susie into the kitchen where she was putting lots of shopping into cupboards. Of course we got under her feet and she had to look down all the time in case she tripped over us. When she had finished she said 'Now it is time to relax and put on a swimsuit'. Panda and I followed her into the big bedroom and jumped on to the big bed while Susie changed her clothes, and then we followed her out through the sliding doors. I was most unhappy to see her walk down the steps into the big pool of water, and then she was covered by the water and she moved up and down from one end to the other, saying 'Don't look so worried Mr D - this is wonderful' and she laughed.

I sat as near to the edge as I could, but Panda was finding it too hot and she sat in the shade under the table. After a while Susie climbed back up the steps and wrapped herself in a big towel. She sat on one of the beds and I hurried to join her, but she was all wet. She said 'You can have your own sunbed, d'Arcy darling' and she lifted me on to the bed next to hers and covered me with a big towel. It was lovely relaxing there and I soon fell asleep for a while. When I woke up I didn't know where I was and it was dark and I shouted loudly.   Susie quickly lifted up the towel and stroked me and said that everything was all right. Goodness, that was shocking. For a moment I thought I was back in that big frightening room again.

I hurriedly jumped down from the sunbed and went back into the house and into our room. Panda was asleep in her bed and I climbed into mine. Susie followed me into the room and said 'It's okay Mr D, everything is all right. I know it is all very new for you and you have been so brave. You have a nice sleep there with Panda, and I'll wake you up at teatime.'

When Andrew returned later he had an arrangement of beautiful flowers for Susie. He said with a smile 'For the Vice President from the President of Sarasota Enchanted Florist'. He added that the flowers would not be fresh enough to sell in their shop after the weekend. Susie said that from now it would be wonderful to have beautiful flowers in her home all the time, because it was the best thing about owning a flower shop.

☆   ☆   ☆

We soon settled into our new routine in this interesting home. Gradually we became more confident and learned our way round. I always went out first thing in the morning and leaned right over to drink from the swimming pool. Susie or Andrew always watched carefully when I did that, and as the days went by they accepted that I could do it without falling into the water. Then I had my morning walk all the way round the pool and then back in ready for my brushing.

As the days went by Susie and Andrew introduced us to some of the local residents – both human and other varieties. Whenever friends arrived at the house we were introduced and the people were very kind and always made a fuss of us. Panda loved being picked up or sitting on anyone's lap, but I only wanted Susie to hold me, and she was very protective when I was introduced. Over the weeks Joan and Virginia came to visit quite often, and Butch and Gary also came to see us, and we remembered them all from their visits in England. Butch was especially friendly and Panda loved sitting on his chest and purring loudly.

Ron

All the visitors enjoyed the view from the house. Beyond the pool was an area of grass and then a big lake. Quite often a large heron, that Susie said was called Ron, would be standing quietly watching the water. We also saw big white birds, some with thin sharp beaks and some with very large beaks, and lots of smaller varieties of birds and ducks. We were also fascinated by a medium-sized bird, which Susie said was Anna the Anhinga. This bird swam under the water in the lake and then came up with only its neck and head showing, so it looked like a snake in the water. Often Anna had a fish in her mouth and gobbled it down. Then she had to come out of the water and struggle up the bank on her very short legs, and spread out her wings to dry in the sunshine.

One of the strangest noises that we heard out by our lake was made by a big bird called the Sand Hill Crane. This bird and its mate always flew in one direction in the mornings and while they flew they called out in such a loud cackling noise that they could be heard over a great distance. In the early evening they would come flying over us in the opposite direction going back to their home, making the same strange loud noise. Sometimes during the day they would come walking along the grass outside our pool area. They walked with a very delicate step as if they really did not want to get their feet dirty. They often stopped and pecked away at the ground for grubs pushing their beaks deep into the earth. I decided that I was very glad that I am not a Sand Hill Crane. It must be a very hard life trying to find enough grubs and worms not to feel hungry, and having a very dirty beak all the time.

The Sand Hill Cranes

On one occasion Susie and I were fascinated to see two of the Sand Hill Cranes dancing. They jumped high in the air with their wings spread out and then they bowed to each other, and then one of them twirled round and round. It went on for ages and then they suddenly stopped and walked off together.

One evening during the first week in our new home Susie called to Panda and me to come outside. Andrew was already out there and he picked up Panda and Susie picked me up. They walked us to the screen and Andrew said 'There he goes, there's Big Al. Can you see him?' We looked out at the lake and saw a long black shape in the water swimming slowly by. Susie said 'That is our resident alligator, and he is very big and little cats must not go near him.' We all watched as Big Al arrived at the opposite bank of the lake where it was quite narrow and not very far from us. He waited in the water for a while and then clambered up the bank and flopped down on the grass. Boy, was he big. Out of the water he looked enormous. I thought 'Oh my goodness, I have no intention of going anywhere near that frightening creature.'

Big Al

As the weeks went by we became used to seeing Big Al cruising by, and we weren't so frightened of him. Susie and Andrew made sure that one of them was always out by the pool when we were out there – just to make sure that we did not come to any harm. We also became familiar with the resident birds that lived on our lake as the same ones came by most days, and there were also strange creatures called turtles. They liked to sit in groups on the grass at the edge of the lake. It was interesting and different. We missed Andrews Reach and all the boats going by on the river, and the people and dogs on the opposite bank, but there was plenty to see and do here too. Pandora especially enjoyed catching Leonard the Lizard, the gecko that lived in the pool area. She would suddenly come hurrying into the house with him in her mouth, but she had to tell us, so that meant opening her mouth and he of course escaped, usually dashing under one of the sofas which meant an exhausting search with all of us joining in – and two of us getting in the way!

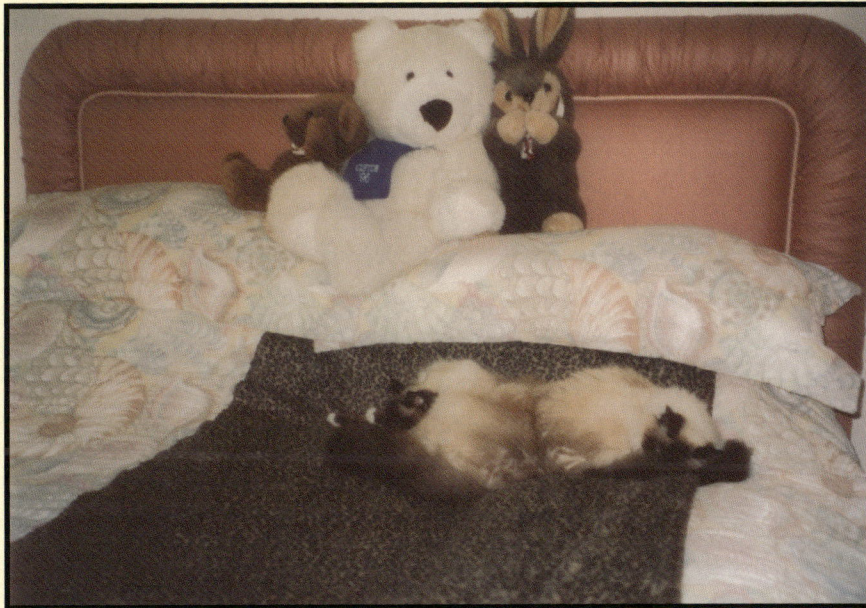

Book Ends

I have to admit also that as we were getting older now we found that we slept for long periods. We had our routine of sleeping most of the morning, often on the big bed in Susie and Andrew's bedroom, although I was quite partial to a nice place right at the back of their closet where I felt very safe. Susie and Andrew had to remember to leave the sliding door open a little so that I could come out when I wished.

We often had a walk out by the pool in the middle of the day. Pandora usually went back into the house afterwards, and I often rested under my towel on my sunbed when Susie was relaxing on hers. In the afternoons when Panda and I were in the house on our own we were often asleep on the big bed all curled up together. As always I liked the evenings best, especially when Susie and Andrew were at home together. After they had dinner we would often go into the den and all pile on to the big sofa and relax whilst Susie and Andrew read books or watched the magic box. Pandora loved to climb up Andrew's chest and sit gazing adoringly at him and giving him head rubs with lovebites on his nose or his ears if he wasn't quick enough. I was always snuggled as close as possible to Susie.

☆   ☆   ☆

One morning Pandora and I were alarmed to see our big carrier on the floor. I noticed that the door to Susie and Andrew's bedroom was shut, so we couldn't run and hide under their big bed. Pandora and I sat next to each other motionless and worrying about what was about to happen. Then Andrew picked me up and put me into the carrier, saying 'In you go, Mr D, you are off to meet your new vet'. Then he picked up Panda and put her into the carrier too. It was a short drive in the car to the Animal Hospital and when we arrived Susie introduced us to a very kind lady called Vicky. She admired us saying that we were very beautiful and that they did not have many Birmans. She wrote down all our details, and then we waited for our appointment.

There were three cages in the waiting room stacked one on top of the other, and inside were three cats. They apparently needed homes. Susie was talking to them and stroking them through the bars. I was shocked when she said that she would like to take them all home with her. I didn't think that was a good idea at all. Fortunately she was just feeling sorry for them, and it was sad to see them in their cages. There was a black cat in the top cage and a tabby in the middle one, and in the bottom cage was an enormous pale ginger cat. Vicky said that the ginger one was on a diet as he was somewhat overweight.

When it was time for our appointment we were carried into a room and I was taken out of the carrier first and put on to a table. The vet was called Dr Whitlock and she was very gentle with me and examined me all over and took my temperature, which was a very undignified procedure! She declared that I was a very healthy handsome boy. Then it was Panda's turn. She was quite friendly at first, but then very cross when it was her turn to have her temperature taken. She was also pronounced to be a very beautiful healthy girl. Our appointment was soon at an end and we returned home. Susie said that it was good to know that we had such a nice Animal Hospital nearby.

☆ ☆ ☆

One day a few weeks after we had arrived at our new home, Susie told me that Andrew had to go back to England soon for a week and that it would just be the three of us, and we would have to be very brave and look after each other. She sounded a bit anxious when she said it, because it would be the first time that she would be here without Andrew, but it made me feel very important as I knew that I would be in charge of looking after Susie. When I thought about this news, I realised that Andrew would have to travel in the frightening noisy huge room again, and I was so glad that we weren't all going too.

On the day that Andrew left he said 'Be good, and I will be back soon' and he kissed us all. That night I prayed to the Goddess Tsun Kyan Tse for Andrew to come back safely, and I also asked Raphael to help me look after Susie. In the early hours of the morning a wonderful thing happened - Raphael appeared suddenly in our room and

Panda and I woke with a start. It was so amazing to see him again and we felt greatly comforted. He smiled at us, and passed through the door.

In the morning when Susie came to wake us up, she was smiling and she said 'Well, guess what - Raphael was here last night. I felt those three cool breaths on my cheek, and when I woke up there was a small white feather on my nightstand. It is such a comforting feeling – everything will be all right.' I gave Panda a knowing look and we followed Susie out of the room. Then the telephone rang and it was Andrew to say that he had arrived safely in England and all was well. Susie said that she knew it would be and she told Andrew about the visit from Raphael.

The week passed quite quickly and the main difference was that Pandora had to sit on Susie's chest each evening. After a while Susie gently pushed her down on to her lap, and I was in my usual place snuggled against her hip, and we were all very comfortable. Susie was very excited when the day had come for her to collect Andrew and bring him home. He walked into the house after a long day of travelling very tired, but delighted to be back with us.

Chapter Seven
A worrying time

One evening when I was enjoying a walk round the pool, Big Al came cruising up and stayed low in the water just beyond the grass. He was only a few feet away from our screen, and Andrew was keeping a very watchful eye on him. I had finished my walk and was relaxing. I was looking through the screen at Big Al, when suddenly there was a crash against the screen as a huge bird came diving down from the sky and then away again. Andrew called urgently to Susie and when she came hurrying out, he told her that a big hawk had tried to kidnap Mr d'Arcy. This was very shocking, and Susie was horrified and said 'Thank goodness we have the screen for protection' and she picked me up and held me very close.

We had been in our new home for lots of weeks and we had settled into our new routine and were very happy, but I knew that Susie was worrying about something. I heard her telling Andrew that she was very anxious about who would look after Panda and me while they were away, and he told her not to worry. I was sitting on her lap and she said 'Well, that is all very well Mr D, but I am worrying about who is going to look after you two because next month I have to go to England with Andrew for two whole weeks.' I was very upset by this news. Susie was going to leave me. Would she have to travel in that huge frightening noisy room to get back to England? I couldn't bear the thought of it. I told Pandora and we were very subdued for the next few days.

Then Susie came home one day full of smiles. She told Andrew that their kind friend Joan had offered to have Panda and me to stay in her home for the two weeks. Susie laughed and said that Joan had never had furry friends in her life before, so she was probably in for a very interesting experience. Pandora and I were not sure what to think about this news but we realised that we would just have to accept it.

The weeks passed and then one day the suitcases appeared – always a worrying sign. Susie reassured us that everything would be all right and we would enjoy our forthcoming adventure. She didn't sound very convincing, but it was probably because she had to face the journey to England. The next morning when we were let out of our room and were wandering around the house, we found that the door to Susie and Andrew's bedroom was closed. We knew that this was to prevent us from hiding right under the middle of the bed because we could not be reached there. So this was it – the start of the adventure. The lids of the suitcases were shut and Pandora and I were put into one of the large travelling containers together. We sat and watched while our beds, dishes and litter boxes were gathered up and everything was carried out to the car, including us.

It was only a short drive and Susie talked to us all the way and we replied in small worried voices. When the car stopped everything including us, except the suitcases, was loaded on to a big trolley and wheeled into a building. We then entered a small strange room and Andrew pressed a button and the room started to move upwards. Susie said that she could never live here because she was so scared of lifts and would never be able to go up and down by herself. That didn't fill me with confidence, but the trolley was soon being pushed out of the room into a hallway. Susie pressed a button on the wall and a bell sounded and a door opened and there was Joan. She was very welcoming and showed us all through to a room containing a sofa and other pieces of furniture, and the door was closed. The sofa was covered with a large towel and our beds were put on to it. All of our other equipment was arranged in the room and then we were let out of our container.

We immediately started to explore the room and I jumped on to the sofa and into my bed and Pandora did the same. We sat there and washed for a while, and Joan cooed over us and told us how beautiful we were. Then the door to the room was opened and we all went out into the rest of Joan's home. Panda and I took our time exploring every corner, while Susie gave Joan instructions on how to feed us and deal with our litter box.

I was on my way from the kitchen into the dining room towards the big windows when I suddenly froze. There was nothing on the other side of the windows and I realised that we were high up in the sky. Andrew came over to me and said 'How about that view Mr d'Arcy – we are on the eighteenth floor – look at all the boats in the Bay.' I moved slowly to the window and looked out. Far below us there were cars travelling on a road and then grass, and then a big expanse of water with lots of small boats and some low buildings in the distance. It was astonishing to see so far. I am lucky to have very good eyesight but Pandora cannot see as well as me. She came to join me and we sat very still taking in this incredible sight. It was very unnerving to be so high and after a while we decided to move backwards away from the window. Joan laughed to see us reversing, and said that she used to feel exactly the same but she soon became used to the height. We decided to go back into our room for a while and both of us jumped into bed and started washing.

It was soon time for Susie and Andrew to leave and they came to find us in our beds, and asked us to be very good for Joan and said how much they would miss us. They stroked and kissed us. They said 'See you in two weeks'. I know Susie was as upset as I was, but Joan told her not to worry and that we would all be fine. Pandora and I decided to take a nap, as it had been an exhausting afternoon.

The next two weeks went by slowly. It was interesting staying with Joan and she was very kind to us. She had lots of visitors who all admired us, and the visit went quite well, except that we were both sick on her carpet at different times, which did not go down at all well. Joan was not used to having to deal with fur balls, and a litter box. I think by the end of the two weeks, she had decided that having us to stay was an interesting experience but one that she did not wish to repeat. She was delighted when

Susie telephoned to say that they were back safe and sound and would be coming to collect us in an hour.

It was so wonderful to be woken from our morning naps by the sound of Susie and Andrew's voices, and we immediately sat up in our beds ready to be picked up and cuddled. I gave Susie several licks and then snuggled into her neck, not wanting to move from her arms ever again. We were so excited and everyone was talking at once whilst our luggage was packed up. I was suddenly alarmed because I heard Susie telling Joan that she had had more surgery in England and she had had serious internal bleeding again. She said that it had even been uncertain for a few days as to whether she could travel back here, but then the surgeon fortunately decided that she could. It had all been so worrying because they wanted to get back here so that we could go home and Joan could stop looking after us. Joan said that was not important, but what was important was that Susie was well. Andrew was taking great care of her, and warning her not to lift anything.

Susie resting

They thanked Joan for her kindness and offered to have her carpet cleaned, which she declined, and then it was time for us to be put into our container again. We didn't mind this time because we knew we were going home. It wasn't long before we were back at our house and being let out of the container, but then the worrying began. Susie was certainly not well. She was exhausted and had to rest on the sofa. Andrew covered her with a blanket and then Pandora jumped up and settled down on her and then I did the same. We wanted to be as close to her face as possible, but Andrew said 'You two will have to move down a bit', and he repositioned us on Susie's hip and legs. He said 'We have to look after Susie at the moment and no-one is to sit on her chest.'

She rested all evening and Andrew looked after all of us until bedtime. He unpacked the luggage and heated some soup for their evening meal. The next day Susie was worse. Her breast was very swollen and she told Andrew that she thought that the internal bleeding had started again. He decided that he should take her to the hospital emergency room. I was frantic with worry at this news and kept getting under their feet. Susie tried to reassure me that everything would be all right and they would be back soon. While they were out Pandora and I stayed in our beds and tried to relax, but I kept worrying about Susie.

Eventually they returned and Susie again rested on the sofa. Andrew said that it would be good to see the surgeon the next day who had been recommended by the doctor at the hospital, and that she must be very careful until then. We all had a very quiet day and three of us slept most of the time, with Andrew looking after us.

While we were relaxing Susie told me not to worry. She said that she knew that everything would be all right because Raphael had been with her again in England. She said that one morning a few days after the surgery they had had a crisis because she was bleeding and they had run out of dressings. She was very worried at the time, as it was a Sunday morning and they had to find a pharmacy that was open to buy more dressings. It was very cold and she put on her long warm winter coat and put her hand into the pocket and there was a small white feather. Susie said that it was the most wonderful comforting feeling. I felt better after she told me this and I prayed that Raphael was still watching over Susie, and I had a word with the Goddess too.

The next day Andrew took her to see the surgeon and it was decided that she should have some more corrective surgery, but it could not be done for four more days because it was a holiday weekend. It was an anxious time but eventually the day came and they left early in the morning. We settled down to wait and they were back in a few hours. This was the first time that Susie had had surgery in this country and it was so surprising that she did not have to stay in the hospital for several days.

When Andrew brought her home she was quite dazed and immediately went to bed. The door was shut and Andrew told us that she was fine but we must not disturb her. I sat outside the bedroom door for ages until Andrew picked me up and carried me to the sofa reassuring me that Susie would be fine. He opened the bedroom door to check on her and closed it and I wasn't quick enough to get into the room, but when he came out again I was ready and I quickly ran in and jumped on to the bed. Susie was asleep and Andrew lifted me up and carried me out of the bedroom. I protested, but he said 'She has to rest for a bit longer Mr D. You can join her when she wakes up.'

Susie recovering

In the evening Pandora and I were allowed into the bedroom and we tried to climb all over Susie. Andrew moved us and said 'You see, that is why you were not allowed in earlier. Now be good and just sit next to her, not on her.' Susie reached out and stroked us. Panda moved in as close as possible and curled up and I rested my paws on Susie's arm, which was very comforting.

Over the next few days Susie started to recover. The surgeon had given her a tight elastic bodice to wear and she had a very small soft drain bottle, which was so much easier to cope with than the huge drain bottles that she had to put up with in England. She had to see the surgeon several times and everything went well and the drain was removed quite soon. Gradually she could do more and as the weeks went on life returned to normal. Thank goodness that worrying episode was over.

Chapter Eight
Florida Wildlife and Uncle Butch

It was very fortunate that Susie had made a good recovery this time because soon Andrew had to leave for England again. I didn't mind because I knew that I could look after Susie, and she said that she felt more confident this time as she was feeling stronger.

One day whilst Andrew was away and I was having my usual lunchtime perambulation round the pool in the sunshine with Susie in attendance, Big Al suddenly came up out of the water just near our screen with a large turtle in his jaws. He moved up the grass and then flopped down. Then shockingly he started to crunch the turtle. Susie said 'Oh Mr d'Arcy – this is so awful, but there is nothing that we can do for that poor turtle' and we hurried into the house. Susie turned on some loud music so that we did not have to listen to the crunching. The following week Big Al did the same thing with a long black snake in his jaws. Susie said that she did not feel quite so sympathetic that time. Anna, the Anhinga, was sitting on a post nearby drying her wings and watching Big Al carefully.

When Andrew returned he and Susie had a very busy time that particular weekend. The occasion was Valentine's Day when apparently florist shops are frantically busy because everyone sends wonderful flowers to their loved ones. Susie had to be careful not to become exhausted and risk any bleeding complications, but she told me that she enjoyed driving the delivery van and Andrew carried the arrangements to the houses. People were so delighted to see him standing there with beautiful flowers for them.

☆　　　☆　　　☆

The following month I had a very anxious time because both Susie and Andrew had to leave for England for four whole weeks. I was very unhappy about this and so was Susie, but fortunately kind Uncle Butch was able to move into the house to look after Pandora and me. Uncle Butch was a very jolly man and Panda adored him. He was very patient and gentle with us, and loved it when Panda climbed up his chest and sat there gazing at him and purring loudly. I was a bit more reserved but I did let him stroke me and gradually I sat nearer to him on the sofa in the evenings.

Uncle Butch gave us our breakfast each morning and brushed us, and then he went off to work for the rest of the day. As usual, now that we were older, we slept most of the day, and then we were excited when we heard him coming back into the house each evening. He often had bags of shopping, and we both got under his feet in the kitchen while he put everything away. Then it was time for our tea, and his first Martini. He chatted to us all the time, and gave us messages from Susie and Andrew. He said that they were missing us so much while they were in England. They were staying at Andrews Reach and we could imagine them feeding the Swan family and the ducks and coots, and watching all the activity on the river. Uncle Butch told us that it had rained every day so far and Susie and Andrew could not wait to get back home to us and to see some sunshine again.

Uncle Butch was a very sociable fellow and a wonderful cook. He often had friends visiting at the house including Gary, who we remembered from their visit to The Dolls' House during our last summer there. Towards the end of the four weeks, Uncle Butch told me that it was my fourteenth birthday and he made me a special cake with a candle on it. I was a bit surprised by this, as I had never had one before. He blew out the candle and said that he had wished that Susie and Andrew could return safely from England.

Uncle Butch's wish came true, thank goodness, and we were so excited when we heard Susie and Andrew arriving. I was beside myself with joy when Susie picked me up and held me close. She had tears on her cheeks and I licked them off. It was so wonderful to see her again. She said 'Oh Mr d'Arcy I have missed you so much.' Andrew was holding Panda and talking to her. Susie said that it was so cold in England and so dreary with all the rain every day. She said that the River Thames had broken its banks and was creeping up the grass and the Swan family could just walk out of the water and up to the balcony to be fed their bread. She added that it was so wonderful to be home in Florida again with us and to feel some warmth.

Kind Uncle Butch had left a delicious meal in the refrigerator for Susie and Andrew, which they thoroughly enjoyed, and after unpacking the luggage it was time for bed. In the morning I heard Susie moving about very early, and I called out to her. She opened our bedroom door and picked me up, and Pandora went through to join Andrew in bed. Susie sat at the computer for ages with me on her lap while she answered emails from friends. There was one from Christine and Nick, the upstairs neighbours at Andrews Reach, to say that the river had gone back down and the moorings were visible again.

Susie and I went out to sit at the pool table, and she said 'You know, Mr D, it was lovely living at Andrews Reach on the river, but this last trip convinced me that we have done the right thing to come here. It was so cold and miserable all the time we were there, and now here we are sitting outside in the warmth in the early morning. We are so lucky.'

☆   ☆   ☆

During the time that Susie and Andrew had been in England, there had been a bit of a crisis at the Florist Shop, as the manager had had to have urgent hip surgery and was going to be in recovery for several months. Fortunately a friend called Shelagh from

England had agreed to come to help for a couple of weeks whilst another member of staff was on vacation. This was very good news for Andrew for the running of the Florist Shop, but not such good news for Pandora and me because Shelagh would have to move into our room. In fact all the time that Shelagh was staying in the house with us Panda and I had to sleep in the small utility room. The problem was that the house was open-plan and so this was the only solution.

Susie made it as comfortable as possible. Our beds were put on top of the machines and there was a chair that we could jump on to, and then it was another jump from the chair into our beds. We soon became used to this new arrangement and the time passed quite quickly. Shelagh was very friendly and said how much she enjoyed the life with us. Andrew said that she worked very hard in the Shop, so it all worked out for the best, but we were very glad to have our room back when she had gone back to England.

Fortunately things settled down in the Florist Shop and after several weeks the manager was able to return to work, just in time for Mothers' Day in May, which was the next big family celebration in the year, and a very busy time for florists.

As the summer went on we became used to the afternoon thunderstorms that occurred frequently. Panda and I did not like the loud noise of the thunder and lightning and we often hid under the big bed until it stopped. The weather here was very different from living at The Dolls' House and Andrews Reach, when we had lots of light rain and dreary grey skies, sometimes for days on end. Here we had dramatic storms and when they were over the lovely sunshine and blue sky would appear again and it would feel very fresh. Sometimes it poured with so much rain that the swimming pool would fill up and I would not have to lean over very far to have a drink.

Chapter Nine
Without Susie

A few weeks later a nice neighbour called Dorothy had arrived to ask Susie to look after her cat and the fish in her fishpond, whilst she and her husband Ray were away for three days. Susie enjoyed looking after Candy Man. She told me that he was a beautiful black Persian, but not as beautiful as me of course. She went each day to feed Candy Man and the fish. However on the second day she came back very concerned as one of the fish had died and was floating on the surface of the water, and Candy Man had been sick on the carpet – all very embarrassing when looking after someone else's pets.

The next day Dorothy and Ray called to say that they had arrived home and had read Susie's note about the events in their household, and had laughed about her embarrassment over the dead fish. This was a relief to Susie, and Dorothy offered to look after us at any time in the future if Susie and Andrew were going away. Then I heard Susie say the most shocking thing. She told Dorothy that she and Andrew were going to England for Three Months !!!!!! and she was desperately worried about leaving the cats for that long and she had been trying to find someone to move into the house to look after us. Dorothy immediately said that she would look after us. Susie gasped and said that it would be too long and a burden for her, but Dorothy assured her that she would thoroughly enjoy it. Susie was so relieved and gave Dorothy a big hug, but I was still in shock and horrified that Susie was planning to leave me for weeks on end.

Susie telling me that she has to leave me

After Dorothy and Ray had left Susie cuddled me and said 'I am so sorry that I have to go away for such a long time, d'Arcy darling. I have no choice as we have to go back to England in a few weeks' time, but I don't know how I will be able to leave you and Panda. At least I know now that Dorothy will look after you, which is such a relief.' When Andrew came home, Susie told him about Dorothy's offer and he was so relieved too.

During the next few weeks Panda and I both had lots of extra cuddles, but we were both very upset and unsettled about the prospect of being without Susie and Andrew. We could not imagine them being away from us for such a long time. We felt very miserable and then another awful thing happened.

Big Al ate Anna !

Susie and I were out for our evening perambulation around the pool and the Anhinga was drying her wings as usual at the edge of the water just below our screen, and Big Al suddenly came up out of the water and took her. She squawked and Susie screamed, but there was nothing that could be done to save Anna. It was so shocking, but I always thought that it was a terrible risk for Anna to dry her wings so close to the water knowing that Big Al could be anywhere. That really put a damper on everything and we were all miserable that evening.

The next day Susie had a call from Dorothy to say that she had a friend who liked cats, and who would be happy to move into our house to look after us for some of the time that Susie and Andrew would be in England. Susie was delighted and Dorothy brought her friend Catherine to meet us.

The weeks went by and Susie and I became more and more miserable.   I felt as if I was going into a decline when the suitcases came out. This was it, and there was nothing to be done. I had to accept it, but once the lids were closed on the suitcases Panda and I crawled right under the big bed and stayed there. Susie and Andrew had to bend down and peer under the bed to say goodbye to us. After some time we came out and looked around. Yes, they had gone.

In the late afternoon Dorothy arrived to give us our tea. She made such a fuss of us and told us we were so beautiful. She sat on the sofa and Pandora jumped up and sat next to her. I stayed down on the carpet. I was just so sad. Dorothy told us that everything would be all right and she would enjoy looking after us. She came back in the evening with her husband Ray. They had come to put us to bed, and after they had carried us into our room amazingly they sang to us! Dorothy laughed and said that it was a lullaby to soothe us and send us to sleep. It was so funny and so unexpected to hear them singing to us that it did make us feel a bit better.

Dorothy was very kind and after a few days we did get used to her taking care of us, but I still had sadness in my heart. I was worried that Susie would not come back to me. Dorothy gave us messages that she had received telling us that Susie and Andrew were safely in England and that they were missing us so much, and that helped, but I still worried.

Gradually the time went by, and then Catherine moved into the house for the last few weeks, so we had more company, which was nice. Catherine enjoyed being out by the pool and swimming so we resumed our walks all round the pool in the mornings and evenings when she was at home. It was too hot for us to walk round the pool during the middle part of the day and we found that we often slept during most of the daytime.

Our new Anna

Then one day a nice thing happened. A new Anna came to live nearby. At first Ron, our big Blue Heron, squawked at her and she flew away, but she came back after a while and sat in the tree looking at him. The next day she ventured down to the water quite near him and he didn't seem to mind. They both sat looking at each other for a while which was quite funny, and then Anna dived into the lake and came up with a fish in her beak. It seemed that it was a peace offering because she gave half to Ron and he gobbled it up.

After a few weeks Catherine moved out of the house and Dorothy resumed looking after us. She told us the exciting news that Susie and Andrew would be home very soon. She said there were just a few days to go. We began to get quite excited but I didn't want to raise my hopes, and then one day Dorothy said that Susie and Andrew would be home the next day. Then I was so excited. Panda was too. We didn't know what to do with ourselves all the next day, and then in the evening suddenly the door opened and there was Susie. I was beside myself with happiness, but I pretended to be aloof – until Susie picked me up and then I just kissed her and kissed her. It was the most wonderful moment.

Andrew came in with the luggage and immediately picked up Pandora. He sat on the sofa and she sat on his chest and gazed at him purring loudly. They told us how much they had missed us and that it was so wonderful to be home. During the rest of the evening we followed them around the whole time whilst they unpacked the luggage and cooked dinner. I woke up several times in the night and then remembered that Susie was home and I went off to sleep again with a feeling of deep contentment.

The next day Susie and I were sitting out by the pool, and she told me that she had been in hospital again in England. She said that she had been to see her surgeon for a check up and he had found another problem, which had to be removed. She said 'Oh Mr d'Arcy, I was so scared, and the worst part was having to go back to Andrews Reach after my appointment to tell Andrew that I had to have more surgery. He was wonderful of course and simply believed that everything would be all right, and fortunately it was. I had the surgery and then we had to wait to know if it was more breast cancer, and it was the most wonderful moment when the surgeon had the results and it wasn't cancer.'

Susie added that she should have known that all would be well, because Raphael had been with her again to comfort her the night before the surgery.

I was very shocked by this news and snuggled closer to Susie. She said 'It's all right, d'Arcy darling, that episode is over and I am all healed again, and let us pray that is the end of it.' That night I prayed very hard to the Goddess and to Raphael to look after my Susie. I was so relieved to have her back with me and life was wonderful again.

☆   ☆   ☆

We settled back into our life with Susie and Andrew home again and were very content. Our only concern at this time was that the afternoon storms seemed to be more frequent and Panda and I were often frightened by the noise. We were glad when they died away each time and the noise finally ceased. As the late summer months passed into autumn we became more used to the afternoon storms. Then we heard Susie and Andrew talking about the possibility of a huge storm called a hurricane coming in our direction during the next few days. They watched the man on the magic box talking about the chances of this huge storm arriving and they discussed what they should do.

The next day Susie came home with lots of big bottles of water and lots of other shopping. She stacked the bottles of water on the shelf in the utility room. They watched the weather reports anxiously and the following morning Andrew started moving the furniture around so that they could bring the outside furniture from the pool area into the house. Panda and I sat and watched all of this going on and wondered how big this storm could be.

Andrew told Susie to take our beds and litter box and our tray of food into the utility room, because that was the only room without a window. He said that if the storm did arrive and was strong enough to smash the glass in the big windows we would have to hide in there until it had passed through. Pandora and I went to explore and it was very cramped in there with all our things, and two chairs for Susie and Andrew to sit on.

We waited all the morning. We could tell that Susie and Andrew were anxious. Panda sat with Andrew, and Susie and I sat on the sofa where she could see the weatherman on the magic box. All the blinds were drawn except one so that they could see if the storm was approaching. During the afternoon it became quite windy and it started to rain. The palm trees started waving in the wind and the shrubs were dancing as it increased. Susie asked Andrew if we should all move into the utility room, and he said that we could wait for a while. By now we could see that the lake had big waves, which were coming towards us, and I wondered where Big Al and Ron and Anna were hiding.

It was quite noisy with the wind, and we could hear branches of the trees hitting the sides of the house. This went on for ages and then we noticed that the wind had eased a little. Susie checked the weather report and said that the storm had changed direction and it was turning east. Susie and Andrew stood looking out and it really did seem that the wind was dying down. Panda and I stayed sitting on the sofa and after a while we could see that the lake was calmer and the palm trees were not swaying as much.

It was getting dark by now and Susie turned on the lights and closed the blind. Andrew said that he was confident that the storm would not come back this way now, and we were all very thankful, especially when we heard the next day Susie and Andrew discussing all the damage caused by the storm in other places.

Chapter Ten
New Friends

A very nice lady came into our lives at this time. She was called Doris and was a neighbour. She came to visit several times and fell in love with Pandora and me. When Susie and Andrew went away for a couple of days with some friends 'Aunt' Doris looked after us. She loved to brush us and of course Panda loved to sit on her lap and gaze adoringly at her purring loudly. Aunt Doris thought that was wonderful, so I was very friendly too. On the second day I even climbed up her chest and gave her chin two licks quickly followed by a lovebite, which made her jump.

During that year Aunt Doris looked after us a couple of times and she came to see us twice a day, at breakfast time and to give us our tea in the afternoon. At bedtime another kind neighbour called Joanne came to put us to bed. Joanne lived across the road and was very happy to help look after us. Then in the summer Susie and Andrew had to return to England again for a long time. A few weeks before they left Susie explained that they had to go, that she didn't want to leave us but there was no choice.

Then the day before they left we were introduced to a couple called Margaret and Sandy who were going to look after us that summer. Susie said that they were friends from Scotland and they were able to move into the house for the whole time that Susie and Andrew were going to be away. In fact it did work out very well because they were very kind and adored us. I missed Susie terribly but Margaret and Sandy were always with us. They did not go very far and just loved being at the house and in the pool. They soon learnt our routine and we were brushed several times a day. They talked to us all the time and gave us messages from Susie and Andrew. I felt a little bit calmer this time as I knew what to expect, and I just hoped and prayed that Susie would come back eventually.

One evening whilst Margaret and Sandy were in the house, I was out by the pool by myself. It was dark and I walked over to the far side. I sat down and looked out through the screen and suddenly realised that I was looking up into a pair of eyes. On the other side of the screen was the biggest cat I had ever seen. It was sitting down but it was three times as tall as me with big tufts on its ears. The cat remained motionless but it bared its teeth. I was so scared and I simply froze. I couldn't move. I sat there for what seemed like ages just keeping totally still and staring up at this huge creature. Suddenly Margaret came walking up behind me and said 'Oh there you are Mr d'Arcy' and then she saw the cat and screamed. The cat ran away and she picked me up and held me close. She called to Sandy and he came running. She told him that I had been trying to outstare a bobcat !

Margaret sent a message to Susie about the bobcat and Susie sent one straight back telling me not to try to outstare a bobcat because they are very dangerous and would attack a small cat like me, so then I was grounded and not allowed out by the pool in the dark by myself. In fact Panda and I were kept in the house when it was dark in case the frightening creature came to visit again.

The summer passed and, as promised, my Susie came back and life was wonderful again. Panda was so glad to see Andrew too. Margaret and Sandy said that they had loved being with us and Margaret said that she didn't want to go home to cold Scotland. It had been a very good arrangement all round.

My Favourite Place

Pandora's Favourite Place

When we were sitting out by the pool the next day Susie told me that they would have to go to England again the following summer, but hopefully not for so long. She said that she just wanted to stay here with us, but that Andrew had work to do in England and she had to go too. She said that she was always so sad to leave us, but that was the trouble with living in two countries. She said that she wished she could take us with her, but she knew that we would not like the journey each time. Too right, I never want to go into that big noisy room ever ever again.

☆   ☆   ☆

We were very happy back in our routine with Susie and Andrew again. Pandora and I were a little less energetic as another year had passed and we were even older. We were fortunate to be in good health, just more sleepy! We enjoyed seeing all our regular neighbours each day – Ron and our new Anna, all the Mocking Birds and the Sand Hill Cranes, and Big Al of course. We also had two new alligators visiting our lake. There was a medium-sized one called Alex who was about six feet long, and a smaller one called Aloysius. They only appeared when Big Al was not around. It was interesting to see them cruising by. One day we were very excited to see two otters on the opposite bank. Susie and I spotted them first and Susie called to Andrew. The otters were eating a fish and then they hurried off and disappeared round the corner of the lake.

During one particular week Susie and Andrew were rather worried because they noticed a baby Sand Hill Crane all by itself on the opposite bank. It was probably only a couple of weeks old and it was walking up and down the grassy bank. Susie and Andrew watched carefully and then suddenly the two parents came flying in and landed near to the chick. It was such a relief, and in fact it happened every day for a week. Andrew said that he thought that the parents needed to stretch their wings in flight and had told the baby to stay put. One day during that week the parents had just arrived back, and suddenly one of the parents spread its wings over the baby. Susie said 'Oh my goodness, there's an eagle flying overhead, and the parent is hiding the baby.'

Talking of babies, one day something very strange was happening out in the middle of the lake. Susie and I noticed Big Al cruising along and then we noticed another quite big alligator coming towards Big Al from the other direction. Susie picked me up and called to Andrew and he came hurrying. She pointed out the two big alligators swimming towards each other, and we all held our breath as Andrew said there might be a fight. When they were just a few feet apart Big Al started swimming in a circle around the other alligator, which remained still. This strange behaviour went on for about ten minutes with Big Al swimming in one direction round the other alligator and then in the other direction. Then they were very close together and suddenly Big Al was on top of the other one for a short time and it all seemed very amicable. Afterwards they stayed together for a few minutes and then the visiting alligator cruised off down the lake. Susie said 'Maybe we shall have some baby alligators appearing in the neighbourhood in the future'.

☆   ☆   ☆

Susie and Andrew went away one weekend during that winter and Aunt Doris looked after us again. We enjoyed all the attention that she gave us. Andrew went to England twice by himself during the winter months and while he was away I looked after my Susie.

One day in the spring Susie and Andrew had been out for the morning, and when they came home Susie told us that we were about to have company. She said that a neighbour had asked if the visitors staying with them for two weeks from England could visit us, as they were missing their own cats so much.

The doorbell rang and in came a couple called Adrienne and Tony. They said that they had two Siamese cats in England. They were missing them so much and they were delighted to be introduced to Panda and me. Adrienne sat down on the sofa and Pandora immediately climbed up her chest and sat looking at her. Adrienne talked very softly to her and they immediately fell in love. Tony was making a fuss of me too, and I quite liked him. Then Susie sat next to Adrienne and so I climbed on to her lap. Adrienne was still talking softly to Panda, and Panda was purring loudly. Susie was laughing because it was so funny to see these two having this long gentle conversation.

During their visit it was agreed that they would come to see us again, and then they offered to come to look after us in the future whenever Susie and Andrew had to leave us for more than a few days. Thank goodness the worrying long trips to England that had taken place during the first three summers that we lived in Florida were at an end. The arrangement with Adrienne and Tony worked out very well as they came to look after us several times over the next couple of years. They stayed in the condo at night and spent the days at the house, keeping us company and enjoying the pool. Susie was pleased with this wonderful arrangement and it suited everyone. Adrienne and Tony adored us and we were very relaxed with them looking after us, except that of course I missed Susie whenever she went away, but she always came back after a couple of weeks.

☆   ☆   ☆

One day Susie came home full of excitement. She sat on the sofa and Panda climbed on to her lap and I climbed across her chest and gave her a kiss. She held me close and then gently pushed me down on to her hip. She said that she had just been out with Aunt Doris and they had been to see a big family of Birmans. Aunt Doris had recently asked Susie if she could find a Birman for her in America because she loved us so much, and Susie had found a breeder only a short drive away.

Susie said that they had arrived at the house where the Birmans lived and a lady had opened the door and when they went inside there were seven beautiful cats in the room. It was so exciting and they were introduced to all of them and were able to stroke them. There were even some tiny kittens, which were adorable.

The lady had told Susie on the telephone beforehand that she only had one cat that she wished to re-home. This was a beautiful Blue Birman called Rapsody. She was three years old and of course she had a wonderful Pedigree name, which was Rapsody in Blue du Domaine de la Lumiere. Susie said that she was the image of Portia, and she wanted to bring her home to us, but she was thrilled for Aunt Doris to have her. Susie said "Oh Panda and Mr D, we now have a Portia in our lives again."

I snuggled closer to Susie, and she held my front paws in her hand, and life was purr-fect.

The End

Rapsody

About the Author

Susie Jackson Batty lives in Sarasota, Florida, with her husband Andrew.

They lived in Beaconsfield, England, for nearly twenty years until they moved to an apartment on the River Thames, and then relocated to Florida with their beautiful Birman cats.

Susie had the privilege of working with the late Lord Burnham as his private secretary from 1983 for ten years, and continued with the Burnham Family after his death. She enjoyed her time at Hall Barn, the private stately home in Beaconsfield, where she remained for sixteen years. In 1999 she became ill and her life underwent several changes.

Susie's first book ***The Diary of the Lady from Devizes*** was published in 2004. It is an uplifting story of dealing with breast cancer, and the decision to move to Florida.

Printed in the United States
105239LV00002BA